Introd

All of the stories in this colle
who have a connection to Sa. ___ ....
here, have lived here or live here now, have worked or
studied here or even taken part in leisure activities in the
city. Even if a writer doesn't have that obvious a
connection with Salford, their story is acceptable if they
can set it authentically in Salford.

Thus, many, but not all of the stories take place in this
robust northern city. The call for submissions was in
honour of the Shelagh Delaney Day, 25 November. We
requested work that showed the human experiences of the
ordinary individual and looked for the resonance that
Shelagh Delaney found with the down to earth people
around her.

All of the work was selected anonymously. Students
from the University of Salford selected the longlist of
twenty that appear in this volume. Staff created a shortlist
of eight from the twenty and Charlotte Delaney, Shelagh's
daughter, selected the winner, Neil Campbell. His story
Everything is Seen at Its Best in the Dark was read out at
the premiere of *All About And To A Female Artist*,
composed by Stuart Stevens and performed at the Salford
Arts Theatre by the Salford Theatre Company.

It has been a privilege to work on this collection and
we hope to repeat this process, also launching a collection
for school children.

Gill James, editor

Foreword

Why I chose *Everything Is Seen at Its Best in the Dark.*

I particularly liked the way a brief moment in time is coupled with enough information about the past to tell the tale of a tragedy and its effects on those concerned. Particularly Sue. The description of her regular walk and her regular route, through very ordinary surroundings, is vivid in its simplicity and heart-breaking against the backdrop of grief and loss. The language is uncluttered and used to great effect. I am always interested in the aftermath of an event, how people cope, how they don't cope. This particular story flicked that switch beautifully.

Charlottte Delaney

Salford Stories

Salford Stories

an anthology

Edited by Gill James

Bridge House

British Library Cataloguing in Publication Data

A Record of this Publication is available from the British Library

ISBN 978-1-907335-44-0

This edition published 2016 by Bridge House Publishing Manchester, England

All Bridge House books are published on paper derived from sustainable resources.

Contents

Everything Is Seen at Its Best in the Dark

Neil Campbell

Sometimes in autumn when the ash trees are filled with red berries there are loads of crows among the branches, and evening sunlight filters through the taller trees, spraying the meadow with golden light. Sue always sits at the same bench near the pond so she can listen to the whispering of the reeds. She's seen whole families of herons by that little pond. And it is quiet down there in the late afternoon. From the bench by the pond she can look beyond the river towards the high rise flat where she lives. And from the eleventh floor Denis can keep an eye on her too. Denis has always kept his eye on her, but he doesn't know everything. She has friends on Chiffon Way and Angora Drive, and sometimes she sees them in the Old Pint Pot, but mainly it's just her and Denis.

To get to the meadow she cuts down the cycle route instead of going via Blackburn Street. She has to be careful to cross on the sharp curve of road. On this occasion a car stops for a stray collie dog that clearly has somewhere to be. Sue crosses and looks up at the apple tree in one of the back gardens down there. She's never seen a cyclist on the route and the road is scattered with broken glass. She follows the road round and finds herself by the bridge. She looks down at the swans that gather beneath it. The water is so shallow she can see tyres on the river bed. She follows along the river by the backs of houses, looking upriver at the weir that sparkles and crashes. She takes a right and then a left past the new houses, where a woman tending a newly-laid lawn ignores her as she walks slowly by. The people in the new houses don't seem to know that it is okay to say 'hello'. Sue thinks of how people are in such a rush these days. She was the same when she was younger, but she has forgotten.

She is not out of breath by the time she reaches the bench by the pond. That is the advantage of coming every day. She concentrates, and listens as the reeds brush together. Then she hears the crows calling out. They fly in pairs above the new-mown grass. How wonderful it must be to fly. It doesn't matter to them if a lift breaks down. In a matter of seconds a crow can move from the meadow to the roof of the high rise.

When her boy was young, Sue stayed at home with him. When he was a baby he was wonderful, but on some days the flat could feel like a prison and the panoramic views seemed like a curse. Once, when watching the Telly Tubbies, she thought she might actually be going mad. She had nobody to help her. Lee was so tiring in his need for her attention. On nice days, when he was older, they would walk over to the meadow with a football. If they didn't have the football, Lee would just run headlong into the bushes. Once she thought he was going to end up in the pond, he just ran straight towards it. But he loved the football. She remembered when he dribbled it all the way around the park. Even then he was determined. If he set his mind to something he would do it, and there was never any changing his mind. Denis tried to argue, but Sue just showed support. Sometimes she reproaches herself for that.

The friends who did speak were as bad as the ones who didn't. She came to think that condolences are not for the benefit of the bereaved. At first, she hated the sight of poppies at the memorial on Chapel Street. She didn't say anything. Friends said she'd 'come round'. But the years after that were just a blur of keeping busy. They didn't mellow her. She thought of all that pomp and ceremony.

For her it was a token gesture. And the patterns kept repeating, and year after year they kept sending the boys and girls of Salford overseas.

Sometimes she thinks Lee might still come back. Sometimes she thinks she sees him in the Old Pint Pot, but there are many young men with broad shoulders and black hair. Sometimes she doesn't remember that he wouldn't look so young now. She always sees him as he was on the day he left. That day when Denis was so proud, and the buttons were brightly shining, and Sue smiled though she wanted to cry. Some days she sees him everywhere. She sees him in Denis's face every night and every day, but that is a good thing.

The whispering of the reeds continues. In the vivid light of dusk the outline of the crows seems sharpened. As the day descends, their outline blurs, and soon enough they are flying beyond her sight. She buttons her jacket against the cold and begins the walk back. In the darkness, she can hear the wing strokes of the crows. Looking up at the sprinkled lights of the high rise, she can see a darkened figure in the living room window.

At Adelphi Street she goes right and walks towards the main road. She cuts through the car park and makes her way down the steps and into the Old Pint Pot. She doesn't see the fusilier on Chapel Street, standing in stone. There are no names of any soldiers on that memorial anyway, and she knows nothing about South Africa.

The pub is filled with students. Sue likes them. And they've done up the Old Pint Pot since the last time she came in. They've done a good job with it. She sees Ken and Pauline from Angora Drive. She takes her red wine over to their table by the window. From there she can see the crescent of the Irwell, and beyond that, the moonlight shining across the meadow.

11

Shortlisted

There was such a terrific array of characters, settings, styles and tales. It wasn't easy and I tip my hat to anybody who manages to convey so much in so few words, which is what all of the submissions achieved.

Charlotte Delaney

A Hui Hou Kakou

Lauren Hopes

It was autumn. Dishevelled, ruby and amber leaves clung to the pavement, their vibrant colours darkened by thick mud and bare branched trees swayed in the wind as if dancing to an unheard song. The sky darkened from white to black and Laini Miller sighed in annoyance as the rain began to thicken. The misty tendrils it had been this morning morphing into rain that hissed and growled as it fell. She was eighteen, smart but unenthusiastic, with a face that according to well-meaning relatives could be pretty if she smiled more.

She continued walking, past the heaving restaurants where large families took shelter, overflowing bins and bright signs displaying quirky names for the attractions ahead. Her auburn hair hung in rats tails around her face as the rain infiltrated her clothing – the grey hoodie under her matte leather jacket clung to her head against the downpour, her jeans fused to her legs and her toes aged by the minute as her shoes became water clogged.

When the sky had been greyer than black, she had turned away from Alison's hurt look as the older woman attempted to wrestle Henry into his stroller.

"Wait a minute, just let me put his lordship into here and we'll walk with you." Alison had smiled, wrinkles that had once been laughter lines formed at the edges of her full lips and warm eyes as she grappled with the struggling toddler.

"Nah you're alright," she'd replied curtly, pulling her hood over her head and turning away before she could be forced to stay.

Laini sighed as she reached into her pocket to retrieve

13

her vibrating phone. Casually she flicked the ignore button, noting the ten missed calls and five unread text messages, before pushing it further into her pocket.

Looking up, she saw what seemed to be a wall of blue sheltered by a rotting, wooden structure, the beams starting to sag with age. It looked to be one of those underwater viewing areas yet unlike the others she had seen where sea lions dove, danced and dived through the crystal clear water, or penguins hovered and bounced around to the peals of laughter of happy families, this one appeared to be empty.

Letting her curiosity and numb feet get the better of her, Laini squinted her eyes as she walked closer, looking around in the seemingly empty tank. Staring through the murky glass she saw what appeared to be a sparse, undecorated enclosure, almost like a public swimming pool yet she was unable to see the bottom. Laini leant forward to rest her head against the glass, letting her eyes blur and ache as she stared into the bottomless pool.

Suddenly blue turned to black in a flash of bubbles as a beast appeared from the deep, its mouth open to reveal rows upon rows of bright, white teeth. Laini pushed away from the glass in horror, losing her footing over her heavy feet before slamming into the ground.

"Shit! Fuck" she hissed as sharp flashes of pain shot from her hands. Quickly bringing them up to inspect the damage she mentally cursed at the beads of blood that were starting to appear and drip down her wrists before looking back up at the thing that had scared her so, her breathing quickening in wonder as she took in the black and white beast looming over her.

Standing at 32 foot long the creature could easily have been used as a school bus. Its large body held in the water by two mammoth fins that occasionally twitched and turned along with its tail as the creature rocked with the water. Its smooth, seamless skin reminded her of the tire swing she used to play on after it had been out in the rain, and she was certain that if she could only reach out and touch it the creature's skin would have the same smooth, rubbery feel to it. Lifting one of her hands experimentally, she let out a breath as the creature's eye followed her movement. It was watching her.

Grimacing in pain Laini pulled herself up, brushing the dirt and blood onto her dark jeans before hesitantly approaching the glass. Turning her head she saw a faded inscription on the wall. A few letters missing through the lack of upkeep.

C-me see Hanini the am-z-ng perf-rmi-g Killer Wh-le!

Lifting her hand, she pressed her bloodied palm against the smooth glass. Hanini twitched before turning his body gracefully to face her, his head twisting as if analyzing her handprint.

"Hello beautiful," she whispered, her hot breath catching on the cold glass. The whale lifted his head; opening and closing his mouth, as he looked at the mark her breath had left on the tank. Tearing her eyes away from the swaying creature, Laini reached up with her forefinger to begin gently tracing a small snowflake onto the condensation, Hanini leaning in with interest as he watched her movements. Bringing her hand back by her side Laini couldn't help the giggle that escaped her lips as Hanini appeared to observe her artwork before nodding his head, his mouth opening to release a symphony of whistles, clicks and chirps as if approving of her drawing.

"You like snowflakes too huh," Laini said, bobbing her head as she mimicked him. "Bet you don't see many of those down here."

Hanini continued to click before stopping to blow bubbles. Laini laughed as she rested her head against the glass.

"I didn't think so."

She stood for what felt like an age, her body heavy and numb as she leant against the cool glass watching the whale as he floated aimlessly beside her, only the sound of the rain beating against the ground breaking their friendly silence.

"For the love of…" Laini groaned, reaching into her pocket to stare at her vibrating phone. 11 missed calls. She was in trouble.

"I gotta go," she said softly, smiling sadly as she watched the whale bob his head in excitement. Hanini opened his mouth, sticking his large pink tongue out as he wiggled it at her. Laini returned the gesture before turning to walk away, holding her mobile up to her ear as she dialled her foster mother's number.

As Laini rounded the corner Hanini clicked softly to himself, swimming as close to the glass as he could before falling still, as if waiting for her to come back. When she didn't he fell silent once more, turning away from the glass and slowly returning to circling his pool.

Buried Voices

David Frankel

When I arrive at the house, there are no cheering crowds with welcome banners flying. Just a Marie Celeste of heaped mail and things left undone; uneaten food, unread magazines. My brother has taken anything of value. A square in the dust on the dresser marks the place where the TV had been.

They called me when the old man was dying but I stayed away until I knew it was over. I arrive late for the funeral. The church smells of furniture polish and the scent of cheap hotel soap clinging to the skin of the congregation. I'm glad my father's gone. My bullied mother died years before him and I feel different now. Complete. Nobody's son. It's different for Robby. Now that we're middle aged men I can see just how much he looks like our father. Him and the old man always got on. That apple didn't fall so far from the tree. When he sobs his way through the service he is comforted by family members who barely recognise me.

Once a ceremonial shovelful of dark wet earth has been dumped onto the empty-sounding box, there is an afternoon of false emotion poured out over a cold buffet in one of the pubs frequented by my father. I perform the duties expected of me until I am suffocated by polite conversations with half-remembered cousins. I leave the pub and walk up the street to the bridge over the canal. Our Kid is there already, leaning on the wall smoking a cig. Until now we've managed to avoid each other. Standing shoulder to shoulder, I see he's put weight on. We are both wearing overcoats and it gives me some satisfaction that his is cheaper and makes him look like a nightclub bouncer.

He was always the stubborn one, so it's me that speaks first. "We used to go under this bridge to smoke when we were young. You remember?"

"You've been gone a while, kiddo."

There was nothing here for us when we left school. I took the first ticket out that came along. I bagged a job running errands for a guy from the city. He called himself a business man but he was a nasty piece of work. So what? When you're at the bottom of the pile and someone offers you a hand up, you don't complain about the way they cut their fingernails.

Robby makes a big deal of lighting my cig. We're both making an effort, but there is a long silence as we both look out from the hump of the bridge across the low lying landscape of The Moss.

Neither of us makes any move to go back to the pub. Maybe we both want each other's company again. Like it had been when we were little, when I use to follow my big brother around. All the local kids loved him. They were a little afraid of him too. He was never afraid to use his size to get his own way; a natural leader.

When we were small the estate was still unfinished. Our house was surrounded by a brick shells, concrete pipes and ditches. No fences or security guards back then, no warning signs or hard hats. We loved it. Rolling through the piled sand and running through echoing buildings that still smelled of wet cement, spark-guns flashing in the gloom. He was faster than me, but I was clever. I could always catch him out, jumping out of the shadows, ray gun in hand. But it was always me that had to die in the shoot outs, whether I got him first or not.

Standing on the bridge with him, places and people I haven't thought about in half a lifetime are suddenly real again. Strangely, out of all the faces from our childhood

18

the one I can see most clearly is Peter's. I suppose it must've been my father's death that got me thinking about him; his dad died when he was a kid. But it's not that that I remember most clearly, it's the things that happened later – and the accident, of course. While the other kids that grew up alongside me had faded into the blur of adult life, Peter stayed as an unaltered image of our childhood.

"Do you remember Peter?"

"Peter?" For a moment he tries to evade the subject, but I know he can remember perfectly well. He looks at me and I can tell by his eyes he knows what I'm thinking. Then he laughs, too loudly. "Peter Pissdrink? Yeah I remember. What about him?" His mood is different, still affable but I can sense the defences bristling under his skin. He looks down at the water and rubs the back of his neck where it bulges over the clean white collar of his shirt.

I let the silence hang for a moment before I answer, 'I haven't thought about him in years, but since I've been back it feels like I could turn around and see him coming down the road.' As I speak I look sideways at Robby. I can feel his discomfort as he glances up the street, back towards town and the estate where we'd all lived, as though for a moment he too expects to see Peter.

Peter was the same age as me and the proximity of our homes made it inevitable that we would become playmates. We were never really friends though. That wasn't the way things worked with the kids 'round here. We weren't like the kids in the Saturday morning serials who got each other out of trouble and shared stuff. We played together because it never occurred to either of us not to.

Peter never had a chance. He was a weirdo. Always dirty. Always saying the wrong thing. He stood out, and

19

that wasn't a good thing round here. People here don't like anyone different from themselves. I see it now in the way they behave around me. It's like they have a sixth sense, an ability to smell the residue of other places. The other kids were the worst. They were like dogs; if they sensed fear, they'd bite. They'd chase him until he stopped, all sweat and breath, to take whatever they were going to dish out, unless he found a hiding place. He got good at hiding.

It was Our Kid's fault that Peter got his nickname. We were all out on the playing field one day, sitting against the fence, talking about football, when Robby came along with his mates. He was a bastard sometimes, Our Kid. Him and his gang all thought they were hard. Still do. They joined in the conversation for a while before they spotted Peter.

Our Robby stared at him and said, "What is that yellow stuff around your mouth?"

Peter did have yellow stuff around his mouth most of the time. It looked like he'd tried to suck up soup and not wiped his mouth properly. Peter ignored them and carried on talking about football, even though he knew fuck all about it, but my brother kept going: "It looks like you've been drinking piss. Peter Pissdrink."

Even I laughed when he said it. It seemed funny at the time. Peter was quiet after that. Later someone threw a brick at him and he went home.

As he left somebody said, "It's his own fault. The dirty bastard never washes his face." Was it me? I was always trying to impress Robby.

A twinge of guilt adds to the anger I feel towards my brother. "His name wasn't Pissdrink."

"I don't remember you standing up for him."

The truth was, when we were little, Peter was alright, but as we got older I started to avoid him. It would've been embarrassing if people had thought we were friends. I only let him hang around because I felt sorry for him and I got rid of him as quickly as I could. Sooner or later the others would only start taking the piss out of him so he was better off on his own.

I take a breath and shrug it off. "If people thought I was his mate, it was hardly going to help me get into Cathy Leyland's knickers."

There is, another difficult silence. I shouldn't have mentioned Cathy, but Robby laughs. "You still got your tattoo?"

I roll back my sleeve and show him the faded tattoo I gave myself to prove my devotion to her. I got as far as 'C-A-' before Robby ran off and told dad.

"Dad went mental." Robby laughs.

The C and A have blurred almost together now and faded. I was sixteen the last time I saw her. I caught Robby mauling her tits behind the newsagents. By then I was used to the little betrayals. When he watched me take the beating over my tattoo he had the same expression on his face that he wore when I mentioned Peter.

I stare out, away from the town to The Moss. It always creeped us out when we were kids but Peter often wandered over there by himself. His life was one of evasion; trying to avoid people like Our Kid, but it never seemed to bother him. He was always cheerful, as though something better was just around the corner. But it was a rough place. You could smell the violence on the warm breath that leaked from the factories and schools at the end of each day. It drifted down the gutters and blew down cinder paths with Peter running ahead of it, just out of reach, until he was on The Moss, amongst the fields of beat and the farm houses with black windows.

I turn back to Robby. "He used to come down here a

lot. Do you remember? He was always over the fields."

I'm not sure you can call The Moss 'fields' exactly. The town used to be surrounded by pits. The last closed the year Peter and I were born. We'd see him sometimes hanging around the old workings. We used to tell each other ghost stories about the mines, based on scraps of truth we'd heard about mining accidents and flooded tunnels. But it wasn't the stories of ghosts or the possibility of falling down disused shafts that made the old mines risky. They sat in a strip of land at the edge of town. Unloved and unvisited, out of earshot and beyond the range of the headlights of passing cars. Bad things happened there if you weren't careful.

Peter always said he wasn't scared. He reckoned he had a guardian angel looking after him. He was retarded enough to believe it as well. If he did have a guardian angel it was a crack-smoking sadist. That, or it was always taking the day off, like my uncle Don who, according to my mother, did bugger all and wasn't even any good at that. Peter hedged his bets anyway, just in case. He kept a low profile and ran when he had to.

Guardian angel or not, if you'd been to his house you wouldn't be surprised he took his chances outdoors. I only went there once. It was cold and smelled like a doctor's waiting room; coughed out air and damp magazines. His mother sat withering in an armchair in front of the TV with her bad leg up on a stool. Her glare was exaggerated by her hair; scraped back and tied. Better to spend the day crouching in the angle of a canal bridge, or out on The Moss where it was just him and the faint smell of the town's smoky breath.

He was always talking to himself. Even my gran said he was 'touched'. I always thought it had something to do with his old man dying. He'd been a miner, but he hadn't died underground. Our Kid told me he'd ended up sucking oxygen from a cylinder and died in hospital. Nobody took much notice when Peter's dad died. It was just another thing that made him different from the rest of us.

Our Kid was right. It didn't do me any favours hanging around with Peter, so I saw less of him as we got older. He didn't change much though. I found him once in one of the mine buildings. He was in a brick shed near one of the pit heads. He was crouching over a small fire he'd made from a few sticks and a creosoted plank. He was holding two sausages on a fork above the fire, which was more smoke than flame.

He looked up as he heard my feet on the gravel and said, "Want one?" As though I'd been there all the time. I looked at the sausage, covered in oily residue and the dirty hand that held it out to me. I shook my head and went to find the others. The next time I saw him he gave me his usual witless grin. "They were lovely them sausages."

Things got worse for Peter after people found out where he used to hide. It was me that told Robby. I can't remember why. I tried to take it back, knowing I'd done something badly wrong: "You can't say anything."

"He's a mental. He should be in a home with all the other window-lickers."

"Leave off him, Robby."

"Why? Coz he's your friend? You soft little git."

"He's not my friend."

"So why do you care?"

"I don't, do what you want." That was what I'd said. "Do what you want."

Me and Robby leave the bridge and walk back to the pub in silence. Back at the wake I fake grief and try not to laugh too loudly while I swap stories at the bar. The afternoon turns to evening and there is a sense of anti-climax as people settle for insincere promises to meet up again in happier times and a quiet exit.

Outside, in the car park there is a final conversation with my brother.

"Will you stay at our place tonight?"

"No. I'll stay at dad's house."

"You sure?" He's relieved. I see the weight leaving him.

"Yeah. I'm leaving in the morning anyway."

"So soon? What about dad's stuff?"

"There's nothing there I want. I'll be in touch about the house. I'm sure I can trust you to sort things out." I sense he is waiting for something. Forgiveness perhaps.

As I walk away he is laughing and joking with a couple of our father's friends. I glance back and our eyes meet for a moment. He waves but I can see the same guilt in his eyes that touches everything that passes between us.

After school Peter developed a taste for cheap cider and glue sniffing that left him partly blind in one eye. He got a job pushing a broom around a factory yard and made spare cash buying fags for gangs of feral kids. I think he really did it because he thought they'd like him, but as soon as he handed the cigs over they'd call him a queer and run for it.

The last time we saw him was a year or so after we left school. It was Halloween. We were hanging around the rec. ground. He came over for a chat and then gave us one of his big yellow-toothed grins and walked off trying to whistle. It was as if he knew it would be over soon and wanted to show us there were no hard feelings.

Halloween here was never like it was on telly, where

the kids all had cool costumes and got sweets dished out by smiling old people. It was just us lot wearing batman masks we'd nicked from the newsagent. We fastened our coats around our necks like capes and knocked on random doors until some grumpy bastard threatened to set the dog on us if we didn't bugger off. When we were older it was just an excuse to get pissed up.

The worst kids hunted in packs for stragglers. Our Kid never admitted he'd been there but I knew he was. He kept a low profile for a long time afterwards. Wouldn't look me in the eye. The gang saw Peter on his way home and chased him, fuelled up on lager, out to the edge of town. Plastic faced superheroes pursued him until he was exhausted and when he couldn't run anymore he hid in an old fridge someone had dumped on the waste ground. I remember the fridge. It had been there a long time, lying on its side with its cracked pipes bleeding out fluid into the soil. He must have lain there until the coast was clear, keeping quiet, listening, hoping the gang would go away and find somebody else to torment. Eventually they did, but that guardian angel of his must have been looking the other way again. The fridge's door had a catch on it and Peter suffocated. They didn't find him till late the next day.

I walk along the edge of the estate where we played as kids and past the waste ground where Peter died. It's been built on now. A hundred identical semi-detached houses with families in them.

Everyone I remember from those days has gone; moved away. The lads from school, family, even Cathy Leyland. She got married and moved to a different town when she was eighteen. I'm glad I got out when I did, but looking up the cinder path towards town, for a moment I long for the days before all that happened. When we were just a bunch of little kids and I would sit proudly on the back of my big brother's bike and he would pedal us in a weaving line across the estate to the playing field where Peter and the others would be waiting for us.

Donut

Bradley R Byington

I clenched the phone tightly in my hand as she continued to raise her voice; the cackling of the speaker piercing my ear drum. It was an ugly, old fashioned rotary, but it preserved my brain from the radiation exposure the world still denied.

"...this is exactly what I keep telling you Brandon! A golden opportunity comes, literally, knocking on your door and you piss it away as if you've got some right to be choosy!"

The black acrylic became difficult to grip with a sweaty palm, trying to jump from my fingers like a bar of soap. I kept the sharp edge of the mouth piece away from my face, a remnant of when I'd smashed it repeatedly into the linoleum floor like a hammer.

"...and God damn it you know that money could do wonders for Tia. But you... are selfish! This is exactly why we got divorced."

"Separated."

"Excuse me?"

"Tiffany, we are separated, not divorced."

"...For the moment..."

"When do you think I can come see Tia again?"

"We're too busy. She has her chemo, and I have to work. God knows someone has to pay for all this. I've got to go."

I hung up the phone and loitered around my apartment, square dancing intimately with a bottle of scotch. A few steps later and I'd traversed the cream-white boundaries of my decaying studio. It was a small apartment, but it was cheap. It was also paid week to week, because I'd surely be on my way home any day.

I flipped the pages of my notebooks, examining my work; diamonds, manufactured in methods meant to mimic the natural process. Unlike nature, my diamonds had no flaws. I studied the products of my art intensely, finding peace in my strategizing for improvement. My eyes were tiring by the desk light when another surprise visitor began molesting my door with his fist. I clenched the bottle neck, took a long drink, and opened the door to a grey, curly haired old man with a thick German accent.

"Herr Chandrasekhar?"

"What? It's late."

"Mmm. Yes, 'Brandon Chandrasekhar'. I have travelled a very long way to see you."

His short stature and skinny limbs were rather non-threatening, so I invited him in. Little brown eyes peered at me through thick glasses, whose round black frame contrasted strongly against his bushy mono-brow. He removed a green Tyrolean hat, and began a conversation that would puzzle me tremendously even to this day.

His name was Dr Geiss, which seemed a strong German name, but simply meant 'Goat'. Dr Goat explained he understood my reasons for refusing the previous offer, and that unlike his colleague he was, in fact, the leader of this project. He was a scientist, not a businessman, and yet spoke first about money: "This project is the apex of capitalism; it's future."

He explained to me that he had collected investors, sixteen of the wealthiest capitalists in the world, to participate in a venture into space. This venture required the manufacture of the largest, and clearest diamond ever made. I was curious.

According to Dr Goat, capitalism was suffering. Development in the poorer parts of the world meant that it took his investors decades to earn the kinds of annual profit seen by their contemporaries in the early 21st century.

I thought this space venture might be the search for a 'new world', or that he had a plan to restart the previously unprofitable moon mines for rare earths and helium-3. I was wrong. He pulled a cigarette from the pocket of his blazer and, without asking, proceeded to light it.

"There is validated, by predictions in Einstein's relativity, a phenomenon known as time dilation. Einstein learned that time is relative, and this relativity can be exploited in an important way: when traveling at a very high acceleration, and subject to strong gravity, time is experienced differently than you and I seeing each other now."

Dr Geiss rubbed his half-finished cigarette out directly onto the surface of my table. I didn't protest.

"Imagine you could climb into a special craft that accelerates to a high velocity and travels around, say, an object of great mass. You might spend only one day on this dilated craft, but when you have returned to Earth, humanity will have aged 10, 100, or even 1000 days while you aged only one; depending on the velocity and gravity encountered."

I'd heard this phenomenon was actually true, and that the early GPS systems had to account for this difference in 'aging' in their atomic clocks. In the brief silence I could hear myself breathing loudly and quickly shut my mouth.

"I have developed such a craft. It consists of sixteen individual units, each housing a traveller. These units will be assembled in the outermost limits of Earth's orbit, where they will form a ring I have named the Kosmisch Baumkuchen."

I was again disappointed by the German translation when he told me this meant something like 'cosmic donut'.

"The Baumkuchen will fire an array of advanced lasers into a tritium, deuterium, and hydrogen reaction bead contained within the diamond you will construct for me. Inside, a superdense, rapidly spinning star will form, which, after we have robbed it of its hydrogen by a carbon bombardment, will leave a miniscule black hole. This hole will have the gravitational pull, and counter balancing centrifugal velocity to suspend the donut on its horizon and accelerate it to a time dilation factor of 100."

"How long will they be up there?"

"Forty days; returning to the profits of a decade's worth of investments and interest. Simply *wunderbar.* There will be future trips I am sure."

He jumped up from his chair and replaced his hat.

"Now I must go, I will leave you my card. Do not forget, you will be well compensated; well enough to pay for say, an experimental stem cell transplantation for young Tia. You just name your price."

How had he known about my daughter's Leukaemia? The diagnosis had dissuaded me from accepting any offer which would take me far off during her last six months. It was true, stem cell transplantation offered a chance, but the process was in its infancy, and had only a single digit success rate. But, then again, if my wife had her way, I'd never see Tia again. I quickly picked up the phone, scratching my cheek with it in the process.

"Dr Geiss?"

"Mr. Chandrasekhar, I've only just left."

"I've decided my price... ...a spot on the Baumkuchen."

"Mr. Chandras..."

"For my daughter."

"...This... this complicates things..."

The Salford Manifesto

Karen Kendrick

It was my mate Bertie who first came up with the idea. We had been sitting in the Widow's as usual, putting Cameron in his place and generally being moaning old buggers. Bertie, with his tendency towards mild racism had been lamenting the influx of migrants into the area.

"You know what I think, John," he began, his words fighting through whiskey and mild induced torpidity, "They should send 'em all down south to live in all those empty holiday homes in Devon. You'd soon see the borders shut."

I opened my mouth to remind Bertie of his status as the son of an Irish immigrant but he had moved on.

"What we need is some ordinary folk like you or I to stand in the election. Stand up for normal people." He fixed an unsteady gaze on me. "What about you? Why don't you go in for it? I'd back you."

I dismissed the idea with a wave of my hand and ordered another pint. But the more he drank the more infatuated Bertie became with the idea. Several drinks later he had produced a mini manifesto on the back of a beer mat, plus a list of people who would be prepared to support me.

I awoke the next day in my cheerless little one bedroom flat, fully dressed and lying on top of a pile of papers and beer mats. As I made myself a strong coffee I looked out of the window. The concrete gloom of Salford Precinct was spread out before me, shoppers already milling around like figures from a Lowry. I thought morosely of my old shop; for many years I had been known as 'Junk Jack,' almost a celebrity in my local area.

31

Them were the best years for me; Ann had still been here and we had run the shop together, selling just about everything.

Times got tough for everyone, of course. And these days with pound shops all over the place and a different Tesco every few hundred yards who would want to shop at our little store? We kept our regulars for a while but even they dwindled eventually. Then Ann got ill and I got a letter asking me to sell up. A housing company wanted to knock all the old houses and shops down and build fancy new homes for the middle class.

I said no at first. But when Ann died I lost the enthusiasm for the fight. So I sold up, and came to live here, taking with me two boxes of possessions. A sad, empty flat for a sad, empty old man.

I looked down at the scribbled writing on a beer mat: 1. Register as a candedate. 2. Begin campain. 3. Kick Camron's arse.

I smiled, which made my head hurt even more. I was about to drop all of the bits of paper in the bin when my mobile sang out. It was Bertie. What he lacked in basic literacy he made up for in enthusiasm.

"I've organised a meeting on Thursday," he told me. "Down at the Lion. I'm handing out flyers on the Precinct. We're all getting behind you."

I opened my mouth to tell him no, I was drunk, I didn't want to do this after all. But I said nothing. *I'll just go along to the meeting.* I suppose I was a little bit flattered that Bertie thought I could do this, and it felt good to have something to think about that wasn't connected with what I used to have.

I wasn't sure what to wear on Thursday. I didn't own a suit anymore. In the end I forked out on a new shirt from Tesco to wear with my jeans.

When I arrived I thought nobody was there. The main lounge of the pub was empty, even the landlord was nowhere to be seen. However when I wandered through to the vault I found it teeming with people. Bertie was at the front, passing out hand-written and photocopied political material. He passed one to me without noticing who I was and I read it with increasing dismay.

"Bertie, this reads like a BNP to do list."

"What's wrong with that?"

"My next door neighbour is Indian. I don't want to kick him out. Don't hand any more out. We need to work out our policies properly."

"OK, OK. Hey, everyone.' He placed his fingers in his mouth and whistled. 'Time to hear from the man himself. Go on, Jack."

The loud discordant drone of pub voices became quieter and faded away. Suddenly I was back in secondary modern, an ancient teacher standing before me teaching us the rudiments of public speaking. "Unaccustomed as I am…"

I cleared my throat. "Hello," I said. "My name is John Davies. Some of you might remember me as Junk Jack. I used to have a little shop…"

I felt I was beginning to lose the crowd. "The thing is… I want to make things better. Not for those executive people that are moving in to work on the telly, or to commute into Manchester. For us lot, the ones that don't have nowt. I think it's about time one of us took the scrap to them."

The room was quiet now, so my confidence began to grow. "We didn't have much to start with, and now they're taking what we do have. I want to stand up for the ordinary people, like you Bertie, and Ada, and Joe and everyone else. And yes, the immigrants too. We work like dogs our whole life, just to find that there isn't a comfortable retirement waiting at the end." I forget my nerves as bitterness began to prickle under my skin. "We're the ones who are up at 5am working on the market, or in the factory packing boxes. And when we go home it isn't to a nice comfortable detached, it's to some shitty estate with drug dealers and crack heads. So I think it's time we make Cameron and his crew listen to what we have to say."

I had exhausted my pitiful stock of political aphorisms. It took a moment for the crowd to realise I had finished, but when they did the clapping and cheering was sudden and immense. I grabbed Bertie's pint of mild and finished it in one.

"Oy!" objected Bertie, then shrugged. "You can buy me one back when you're Prime Minister."

The next day we went along to the town hall to return the stack of paperwork Bertie had been given the previous week. We also took along the £500 fee, which we had collected in a bucket the night before in the Lion.

"Robbin' bastards," grumbled Bertie. "That's what I mean about keepin' the common man down. Pocket money to that lot, innit?"

The clerk raised her eyebrows when we placed the bucket of money on her desk, but she was extremely polite. I wished that I had dressed more smartly; I had on a pair of jeans and a T-shirt, both of which were probably older than the clerk. Bertie was even worse; he was wearing an old shell suit which he had had since they were in fashion.

Administrative matters dealt with we began our campaign. We had left it all a little late; the election was less than a month away. I drew up a leaflet I was happy with and Joe's daughter typed it up for us. It looked pretty good when it was done; a happy smiling me underneath the words 'Vote for Junk Jack. He speaks for YOU.' She had tidied up the bullet points I had scribbled down too; I have a tendency to ramble.

We began by knocking on doors in the local area. One of the things I love about Salford is that you're never quite sure what you're going to find behind that door. We made a game of it, Bertie and I, based on the appearance of the house.

"Catholics," said Bertie as we approached house number three. "Look at all the toys in the garden."

He was correct. The next two houses belonged to Bangladeshi families. An elderly Polish woman answered the door after that. We met gay and lesbian couples, drug addicts and alcoholics and immigrants from every continent.

I realised that I was desperately unprepared for the range of questions posed to me by the electorate. What was my stance on abortion? Did I believe in gay marriage? How was I going to tackle the immigration crisis? Did I support food banks?

"Well, I use them if that counts," I answered. By this time I was feeling tired and disheartened. The day's campaigning had been less than successful. All of the residents had conflicting problems and they looked at me as though I was part of the system which was failing them.

The woman who was standing in the doorway looked tired and unconvinced. A child was crying somewhere inside the house.

"My husband can't work," she told me. "They said they might cut his benefits. Just… do something, ok?" And she closed the door.

"Well, you heard the lady," remarked Bertie. "Come on, three more streets to go and then I'll buy you a pint."

As Election Day approached I began to feel uneasy. We were working late into the night writing out political literature and discussing strategies. I was hardly eating, and drinking too much, and my body was suffering. I didn't have time to think about my health, however.

The day before Polling Day we had planned a big rally in Buile Hill Park. We had been organising it for two weeks but I wasn't sure if anybody would turn up on the day, and part of me hoped that nobody would. After all, they were always talking on the news about voter lassitude. Who really cared about politics anymore?

But Bertie, my excellent campaign manager, had achieved a minor Salford miracle: the park was teeming with potential voters, who looked anything but apathetic. My nerves multiplied; I climbed up onto the makeshift podium (two tables pushed together) with my whole body shaking.

Bertie whistled and the crowd grew quiet. I had made a few notes which I held in front of me with a trembling hand.

"Salford has a proud history of political resistance," I began. "Karl Marx and Friedrich Engels used to meet in the pub to discuss the Communist Manifesto. What we want is a new manifesto, for the Salford people." The crowd were beginning to murmur but I pressed on. "I'm not a greedy person. I don't want David Beckham's swanky house or my own yacht. What I wanted was my little shop. But ordinary Salford people are being pushed out of their homes and businesses to make way for posh new houses. We could go and live somewhere else. But why should we? Salford is the birth right of the ordinary people. Someone needs to tell the PM that the people of Salford matter; that if he shuts our libraries our kids won't be able to read. If the government stops helping the poor families they can't feed their children. If you vote me in tomorrow, that is what I plan to stand for."

The blast of applause almost knocked me over with its ferocity. I took a step back.

"You alright mate?" asked Bertie, looking at me oddly. "You've gone white."

That was when I started to feel sick. "I'm OK," I said. "I'll take some questions now."

A thin ferret faced man in a grey suit raised his hand. "Are you an educated man, Mr Davies?"

"I certainly am," I replied. "Secondary modern till I was fifteen."

"And how do you expect to intelligently debate policies with people schooled at Eton and Cambridge with such a small amount of education?"

"I do alright on the pub quiz on a Thursday," I replied. This raised a laugh from the other members of the crowd.

"You'll be a laughing stock," muttered the man, and he walked away.

I was beginning to feel dizzy and my chest was hurting. An Asian man raised his hand.

"Yes?"

"I was recently given this leaflet of yours. How can you claim to represent the immigrant community when you peddle such racist rubbish as this?"

I groaned internally. He was holding a copy of Bertie's handwritten BNP-style leaflet.

"I did not authorise that leaflet," I began. "It was…"

I never got to the end of that sentence because, I am told, at that moment I collapsed.

I awoke in the ambulance, attached to a heart monitor. The paramedic by my side asked me a couple of questions and then told me to rest.

I was taken to Hope Hospital where I was connected to

37

a different beeping and blinking device. After a couple of hours Bertie arrived, looking flustered.

"They loved you!" was the first thing he said.

I groaned. "Bertie, I'm having a heart attack. I think it's time to admit defeat. Besides, they didn't all love me. What about them two at the end?"

"The heart attack was genius. Everyone's on your side now, even that snotty git from the newspaper."

I shook my head. There didn't seem to be much point in arguing with Bertie. After a little while a young doctor approached my bed and asked me some questions about my lifestyle. Bertie bought a couple of papers and we sat in friendly silence as we waited.

Bertie stayed with me for hours. At about 10pm another doctor came to my bed. By this time I had had enough waiting and wondering.

"Have I had a heart attack?" I asked, pathetic, snivelling.

To my surprise the doctor shook his head decisively. "Your heart is as strong as mine," he said. "I hear you've been under a bit of stress lately. And have skipped a few meals?"

Bertie looked at me. "You divvy."

The doctor told me that if my blood tests came back clear I could go. "But what about the chest pain?" I asked.

"I can't say for certain at this moment," replied the doctor. "But my guess would be a build-up of wind caused by a poor diet."

Bertie howled with laughter at this.

We didn't win the election. Labour got in again, of course. But we managed to get 853 votes, almost as many as the Lib Dems.

I feel like Junk Jack again. People stop me on the market now and tell me how their families are doing. I get invitations to tea at least twice a week.

Bertie has plans for me to run for Mayor next, but I think my political career is over. If the Downing St. lot want some policy advice they can always come and find me. I'll probably be in the pub.

The Rain of Salford

Giacomo Perazzi

It was raining softly, but conspicuously; the type of rain that you can't really feel on your skin, but that for some reason still penetrates your bones and chills your insides.

Despite his woolly jacket and hat, Daniel was freezing his arse off. He had sat at the bus stop for the last half an hour, but of the seven buses that stopped in that time none had been the right one. The transparent plastic cover of the bus stop was barely enough to shelter him from the faint rain, which was making his general mood fall down below the asphalt of the road; his jolly nature washed away with the runoff water.

Buses made him depressed; looking at the people sitting down as far away as possible from each other, everyone lost in their own thoughts, everyone gloomily waiting to get to their destination. He really didn't feel like going to work today.

He looked up; no point staring at the road, hoping the bus would suddenly appear. He felt like the universe was enjoying pissing down on his head. He often had that feeling, as if he was the object of some life long, perverted prank.

Different people had waited with him at the bus stop and then left for whatever destination they were going to. In normal circumstances Daniel would have tried to speak to them; maybe offer them a fag in exchange for small talk. He valued what other people had to say, even if it was just a comment on the latest game. But today he really could not be arsed with anyone. Salford had that effect on people, he reflected. It swallows everything up in its greyness, creeping up on the mind like a giant lobster, locking its claws around their neck and slowly suffocating the thoughts. If you are not careful it will bring you down, clouding your soul until you start becoming part of the grey. When you realize it's happening it's too late, you have assumed the same abandoned and deteriorated look of suburbity, with its shabby buildings and sad roads.

A girl walked up to the bus stop and sat on the bench. She was carrying one of those large, flat cases to keep artwork in, and she was wearing a stained blue apron. She smiled at him and he thought she was nice, couldn't be more than three years younger than him. He was about to initiate conversation when she stood up and waved at the bus. As she walked towards the bus that was pulling up Daniel saw something slip out of her pocket and fall to the floor, without her noticing. It was a fabric pencil case with colourful rings decorating it all around. He picked it up and hurried behind her, but at that exact time he saw his own bus finally appearing on the road. That moment of hesitation caused him to stand confused as the first bus closed its door and drove off, and the second one drove past without stopping. He watched the two buses disappear.

He was fuming, so fuming that he threw whatever he was holding in his hand to the floor. He immediately regretted it. The pencil-case had fallen in a puddle on the side of the road. He used his jacket to clean it as best as he could, then he put it in his pocket. He didn't know why he hadn't simply left it in its puddle; it felt wrong for some reason. Somehow it was wrong for that pencil-case to be left on the floor.

He had lost the bus. Now he had to wait at least another half an hour for the next one. It was another mean joke by the universe. That damn girl!... The girl, he thought, she lost her pencil case, so neatly decorated,

41

precious, she must have been gutted. But why should he care? He shouldn't, but nevertheless he did care, and he felt bad for her.

It took him only a moment to decide. That day he wasn't going to work, that day he was going on a quest: the quest to return the missing pencil case.

There were only five stops till the end of the bus line she took, he calculated. She was probably getting off at the Quays. If he was quick he had a good chance of catching her. A wave of excitement was rushing to his head, making him feel alive and good. He used it to work out a plan on how to get there in time. A very ingenious plan. As soon as the taxi arrived at the destination he opened the door and legged it. He felt the adrenaline pushing him faster as he laughed at the very pissed-off driver. Once he was sure he had run far enough he stopped to take his breath. Daniel had ended up in some shady back road, not far from the end of the bus line. He walked towards it and, after reaching the open space of the square, he saw several buses parked up along the pavement. None of them was the right number, and now he felt stupid for the silly idea that had got into his head. What had got into him? What was he trying to achieve? It seemed like his quest was to finish at its start. All the adrenaline and excitement he had been feeling suddenly evaporated from his spirit, leaving him like an empty shell, and with a bit of broken heart.

It was still raining and the rain smelled bad. He couldn't stand that smell. The same smell of false hopes and desperation, full of wrong principles and broken ideals. He looked around; a few people were scurrying around like sickened ants of some diseased colony. He was about to give up when he saw him. He recognized her bus driver from the tattoo on the back of his neck. The man was leaning against a wall, smoking, and apparently oblivious to the fact that he was getting wet. The rain didn't seem to bother him, even though his fag wasn't burning properly. Daniel couldn't believe his luck.

He approached him with a renewed sense of purpose. His instinct had been right, confirmed the bus driver; the girl had just got off the bus a few minutes ago. The driver could even tell him which direction she had taken.

"Lovely lass, she seemed," said the driver as Dan hurried off behind her trail. "I hope you find her." He hoped that too, but he wasn't sure why.

The more he fell into this rushed adventure the more he felt his heart pounding; it was set on a desire for diversion, a need to believe that sometimes you just have to give life the finger and head-butt your way out of its grip. Today was the day of his great escape from the prison of monotony, and he had never felt more alive. Some strange force had guided him so far, maybe with the intention of purging his soul. He felt a cathartic power telling him where to put his feet, and Dan simply had to let it lead the way. A gentle wind started blowing. The air was pushing on the back of his jacket to make him move faster. He was running through the streets of Salford, turning every corner with the hope she was going to be there. Each time he found another street, empty, but he didn't lose determination. And then he was running along the river, lots of vegetation growing freely on the water's side, a sudden dash of green in this grey painting. There was an opening between two bushes; behind it he could see a dirty river bank, under which the water was making its lazy way.

The same force as before was pushing him to cross the gap between the two green hedges; even the rain was bended by the wind in that direction. He already knew what he was going to find on the other side.

She was sitting there, in her blue apron, the colour that the river's water should have been. Like that bus driver, she wasn't bothered by the rain, and she was sketching on a notebook, careless of the pages getting wet. She heard him approaching unsteadily on the stony ground, but she wasn't startled. She simply turned around and watched him come down the bank towards her.

"Hi." said Dan, out of breath from the descent to the river level. The water was now flowing only a couple of meters from where they were.

"Hi," said the girl, observing him with eyes full of curiosity.

"Sorry to bother you. You left this at the bus stop, I thought you might want it back." He pulled the pencil case out of his pocket and offered it to the girl, who seemed genuinely surprised.

"Thank you. How did you find me?"

"I'm not sure myself; I just followed the bus, sort of thing."

"That is amazing. And a bit crazy," she added. "You know there was my address written on the side?"

"Oh." He hadn't noticed it.

The girl moved across and invited him to sit down.

"Are you from Salford?" Dan asked once he was sat next to her. There were white specs floating on the brown water. He could see a couple of ducks, sheltering from the rain on the other side of the river.

"I moved here three years ago," she said. "My family still lives in Devon."

"Do you like it here?"

"It's alright. I guess."

"I hate this fucking place." He threw a stone in the water in annoyance.

"It's not that bad. This city just needs a bit of love."
He didn't say anything anymore and they sat in silence for a few seconds. "How about you?" she finally asked.

"Well…" he laughed. "I probably lost my job now, so I don't really know."

"You serious? Have you lost your job for that old pencil case?"

"It's nothing, really." He laughed.

"Well, for what it's worth, thank you. That was brave, not many people are like that here." He nodded in acknowledgement. "What is your name? Should I call you my hero?" she carried on.

"Daniel, Dan. Just Dan actually."

"I'm Charlie."

They sat looking at the rain creating specs in the water, as the current carried away their thoughts. Charlie had started sketching in her notebook again. Her hair was cascading onto the paper so that he could not see what she was drawing.

"What do you do?" he asked her eventually.

"I'm studying art at Uni. What about you? You a student?"

"No I like to learn from the real world. I simply like to observe and listen; I like what people don't value, it makes it priceless, somehow. I like people and the little secrets this city sometimes offers. I know a lot about its inhabitants."

"What do you know?"

"I know that Ahmed at the gas station will give you a twenty pence discount if you show interest in what he has to say, I know that every Wednesday an old man walks to Peel Park to leave a flower in the river's waters and watch it float away, I know that the lady who lives in that fancy house in the street behind the shops is actually not a lady…"

He could have carried on for longer, but she interrupted him. "You certainly seem to know a lot about people, yet I can't help but feel that you don't like them."

"I have given up hope in people, in this forsaken city. It doesn't mean I hate everyone."

"Why give up on people? You just ran half the city to give back an old pencil case to someone you didn't even know. If I was like you I would have given up on it, yet here you are."

She had a point, he had to admit it. With a smile she had made him question his principles and revealed to him how wrong he had been. Maybe he had been wrong not to trust the universe. She was staring at him on the edge of a laugh.

"Look, here." She said and she showed him her drawing. It was a black sketch of the horizon, a landscape of buildings, reflected on the water. The Irwell on the paper was of the right colour, an intense turquoise that faded into green. He liked it; it reminded him of years ago, when things were easier and the river's water was still blue. Was now too late to make it blue again?

He looked up. Behind the trees, behind the buildings, and behind the hearts of Salford's people, the sun was dusking, painting the sky with its warmth. The rain had stopped.

It was the most beautiful thing Dan had ever seen.

Three In Four Out

Daniel Fishwick

A satisfying slam of the door echoes across Church Street. Through a first floor window I feel eyes on me, congregated office workers in matching white shirts, all snub nosed against the glass. Their faces in feigned shock, contorted in disapproval about something they wish they'd been brave enough to do. My hand begins to swell. The relayed messages hum in my ear as I hear bystander voices. Linda From Finance with her own altered version of events being told to the people who want to matter, those in slightly more expensive white shirts. A fast pulse throbs in my temple, my steps are quick. Calm it, calm it. Shutters rattle upwards sending pigeons with them. Cafés opening but no one to populate them, a few stranded nanas eye up the pound shops and stand firm by tartan trolleys. Usual lack of fanfare for a Tuesday.

Overlooking, overbearing, the town is the church. It's Victorian clock face blocking the lilac and grey sky. It looms over me as I sit below on one of the uneven wooden benches. Perching on the one with the least slats missing I take the chance to breathe, like they told me to, in for three and out for four. In for three. Out for four. For all their talk, it actually works. I feel my heart rate slowing down, my lungs opening and the thud in my head begins to fade. For a moment, brief as you like, it was close to the one thing I never get – silence. Weeks, sometimes months on end, waiting for something as intangible as that, it sends a bloke mad. A book burns a whole in my pocket, only one chapter read. Its neglected pages begin to dog ear while making home in my coat. All those words left unread in favour of work's clock. Small chance to read would be a beautiful thing, a true gift. This appears to be the unexpected time it could happen. Before the shoppers begin plodding, while the birds settle in the bare branches of the trees. No pneumatic drills, no street side sellers. I reach for the book and feel my spirit lift. Like clockwork, the beeping reversal of a delivery van bursts the bubble. The noise sends me to the tram stop, home could be empty, I hope home is empty.

The town's other main monument is the supermarket, at odds with the church as both buildings battle for skyline. A warm wave of bacon air sweeps across the platform. Fare dodging apprentices stroll by the ticket machines. All in Hi-Vis vests, each one wielding a bottle of Lucozade. Bacon rind hangs from the corners of their laughing mouths. A dispute over peak and off peak prices begins to flare up amongst the pension age ranks. And still no silence. The tram reluctantly pulls in. Achingly slow, the big metal slug settles below bright supermarket awnings. As soon as I've found a scat, it begins. The lads bang on the windows in a bid to get the attention of four same-aged pram pushers. They ignore them at first but the braying soon works and the prams begin to follow the path of the tramline, angled towards the next stop. Sure enough, Ladywell arrives and the boys hop off eagerly. The sound of their bottles hitting the pavement, far from a bin, goes through me.

My old man, rest his soul, called this The Warpath. The route you're set on after what could be an innocuous event, the erratic frame of mind that only wants trouble. Doesn't take much. It could be as simple as this morning. As it is, everything grates. The hiss before the automated prompts for the next stop and the electronic voice that follows with all its nasal elocution. The clouds that gather over the precinct ahead, threatening more rain. Stop start buses that clunk alongside the tram, sending passengers slowly rocking back and forth without expression, all passive.

I take the book from my pocket, shift the weight of it from my swollen right hand to my left. With the tram empty, I peel the bookmark away from the page and focus on the first word, blurred at first, becoming clearer, then perfectly sharp. Before the second word my phone rings. Never any silence.

"Dad, don't go mad but I need to tell you something." Sophie says in a voice quiet with panic.

"Go on love."

"Promise you won't go mad first."

"I bloody promise, what is it?"

"It's Hugo. I've lost him."

"How do you lose a bleedin' Labrador?"

"He went ape, I couldn't pull him back."

"Can't Julian go and get him, it's his dog, you've lived at his long enough. Get your Mum to sort it."

"I can't tell them. You've got to help me, Dad. Can you get out of work?"

I look at my swollen hand. "Yeah, I don't think that'll be a problem darlin'. Hold on to something, I'll be round in a minute." I plunge the book back into my coat pocket, where it'd remain for another week.

A distraught Sophie meets me off the tram, all streaky mascara and knotted hair. We start the walk to the Quays together. And we began to talk. About school, about how Mrs. Lewis was a pain in the arse, how Candice didn't listen when Abbie told her she liked Craig, how her Mum wasn't happy on the trip to Tenerife and she didn't know why. Her voice is like music, a loop of delicate sounds, bouncing off each other. Each syllable leaves her mouth with simple swagger. The tone is intuitive, passionate when needed and calm as required.

49

We make it to the Quays. Sleek walkways of reflective paving, almost like marble, guiding people in suits from one glass building to the next. Panes of glass that panel up and across, vast boxes beaming the sunlight backwards onto the water of the Quays. At once both impressive and sad. It's Sophie's presence that keeps it from irking me, I know it is, there is no tension in my shoulders.

Tied to the railings is a happy Hugo. Never lost, never missing. Only an excuse for me to listen, an opportunity for me to hear. Now we get to walk back together. I'm grateful and I never want silence again.

Aare Rivers

Kimberly Walker

KAVERI

"The bridge or the field," asked one of the women. Almost in unison, everyone replied the bridge.

Kaveri was reluctant to join them because she feared the water, ever since a rafting accident that occurred many years ago. After receiving permission from the elder woman to take the path by the paddy field, she pressed her palms together and bowed slightly to bid them farewell.

She journeyed past small towns and small houses, each that were separated by acres of luscious green fields. The endless rows of rice plants swayed along with the evening wind; a light breeze that was of no help to Kaveri as she readjusted the heaps of firewood that sat uncomfortably on her head. After waving to the villagers nearby, she made her way back to the worn-out shed that she calls home.

"Nana?"

Suddenly, a loud screech echoed through the emptiness. Kaveri immediately recognised the scream that belonged to her sister. It was all too familiar.

Dropping the firewood at once, Kaveri ran towards Nana's cry for help. Later, what she saw left her frozen in her footsteps.

He was holding Nana tightly by the neck and dragging her towards the river. Nana's head was forcefully shoved into the strong-flowing current.

"Appa! Stop! Let her go"

"Never. You ruined our family. You brought us bad luck. You shall drown and be with the devils that are your real family."

51

With every ounce of strength left in her weak legs, Kaveri ran and tore Nana away from her father's grip. But the current was too strong to keep her standing. Kaveri slipped and fell into the gushing water, where her fragile body was engulfed by the heavy tide.

YAMUNA

"Girl, what's your name?"

I peeked from underneath the shawl that covered my face, and a young lady was crouched before me with her hands held out. I was surprised because for the past month that I have been living among dirt, rags, and leftover curry, no one has ever approached me. I'm invisible to most people; even the stall owner beside me beats me with a broom like I'm a pest that needs getting rid of.

But this lady, she was kind, just like my sister was.

"What's that?" she pointed at the protruding bump on my forehead.

"Aren't you scared of me?"

The lady looked at me with furrowed eyebrows and shook her head, as though she did not see any reason to be afraid of me. Instead, she pulled out a napkin from under her bright yellow sari and started cleaning my face.

"You braid your hair too," I said as I reached to feel her soft silky hair.

"Yes, it's the first thing I do every morning"

I felt strangely happy upon hearing those words. They sounded familiar, like I have heard them in a different voice before.

"Do you want me to braid it for you too?"

"My sister tried but it couldn't. My hair is too…" I paused as I felt the split ends scratch the back of my palm. "*rough.*"

"Nonsense. Where's your sister then?"

I was silent for a moment because I felt my lips tremble and my eyes swelling up with tears. I didn't want to cry, I wanted to forget. But it was impossible, especially when I was staring into the eyes of a lady who looked just like her.

"What's your name, girl?"

"Yamuna."

"That's a beautiful name. Come on Nana, let's go home."

SARASVATI

She sat by the window with a book that read *India: The Holy Rivers* rested on her lap. As she traced her fingers along the pictures, she found herself on a page titled 'Sarasvati – The Lost River'

"Why did you name me after a river?"

"Hmm? Oh, because it sounds nice," her father replied from across the room, without even glancing over at her.

"But why a lost river?"

"That's just a myth, sweetheart. You can't still believe in myths do you? You're seventeen."

"I don't. But you could have picked a better name though. Like Narmada sounds nice."

He finally stopped to look up from his iPad, as though something triggered his memory. Whatever it was, he snatched the book from her and just then a picture fell out of its pages.

Sarasvati scrambled to pick it up. Her eyes widened as she held up a picture of a man holding a pregnant woman's belly.

"Who is she?"

"Give it back, it's none of your concern"

"I will not, until you tell me who she is." Sarasvati shoved the picture into her pocket and ran to her room.

She stood before her mirror and stared intensely at the photo. She looked up at her reflection then back at the picture again. She did not stop because the woman and Sarasvati shared features that were too uncanny to miss. While her father banged furiously on her door, Sarasvati felt her hands touch her wet cheeks. She knew who the woman was instantly, and the man too. All the years of searching for answers had come to an end. The picture spoke a thousand truths; the man and woman were her real parents and everything Sarasvati knew were beginning to fade into lies.

NARMADA

Despite his muscular physique, he felt small and powerless as he sat waiting impatiently in the corridor of the village hospital. With his head sunken into his wide palms, his worries were multiplying by the minute.

"Congratulations. They're twin girls."

Rajesh looked up and his eyes met with the doctor's tired and worrisome expression.

"What about Narmada?"

The doctor was at a loss for words. Rajesh, who understood what had happened, fell to his knees and broke down in a puddle of tears. He tugged at the doctor's white coat and begged. He pleaded but no words could describe the agony he felt. He cried but his tears could not heal his broken heart. He screamed but no anguish could make his dead wife's heart beat again.

"We have an agreement Rajesh. I hope you are a man of your words."

"You are a monster. How can you stand in front of a

widower and talk about death like it doesn't hurt? I lost my wife. And I'm losing one of my daughters too? Have mercy, Doctor, please I beg of you."

"We agreed on a trade that I would lift the medical charges if you took Yamuna far away and gave me one of the twins. Your wife was not part of the plan."

"But my wife is dead! And you still expect me to get rid of your illegitimate child?"

"My condolences, Rajesh." And with those last words, the doctor and Rajesh never crossed paths again, and neither did his other daughter, whom he last heard was named Sarasvati.

Battenburg

Meg Rowles

Betty Baxter was a cantankerous old soul. Glaring with narrowing eyes towards the murky tide that rocked the wind beaten fishing boats, her sagging face decorated with deep wrinkles continued to lick rather greedily her melting ice cream, that dripped down her fingers and onto her widely open legs. Wheeling her tartan trolley over to the harbour wall she noticed a young boy stooped over his fishing line crabbing.

"Caught anything yet kid?" she yelled, dropping the remaining ice cream onto him. She laughed abruptly, lighting a large cigar which she hung loosely in her mouth. Slowly, shuffling her feet along the sandy pavement towards the busting town, all Betty could see through her circular spectacles was a sea of bobbing heads.

"I bloody hate tourists!" Betty exclaimed.

As she walked through the roar of engines, rude hand gestures were given to the stagnant traffic along with toothless similes and sarcastic royal waves that irritated the solemn drivers and showed her vast collection of golden rings that engulfed her wrinkled fingers. The small market was swamped with bargain hunters. You could see the stall holders, all gasp for breath as the overwhelming crowd surge forwards towards the merchandise. All equipped with large, economy sized shopping bags the tourists, whose white socks went lovingly with their open toe sandals, stood in rows of five like bombarding warriors, in front of other sweaty, red faced battering rams as they slowly sieved through their mounds of copper for that got to have 99p plastic windmill. Meanwhile heavy breaths collided with energetic hollers and persistent screaming children who lay covered in flaky pastry. All this was a perfect distraction for Betty, who started loading Battenberg and fruit scones in the direction of her deep trolley.

"Don't mind me."

She sneered, as she slyly grabbed another jar of pear drops, pushing them into her ever expanding double D's. Backing away, her head once again reverting back to the down-trodden, doddery old woman, she headed towards the town's more lavish boutiques.

Betty Baxter entered 'Oh la la!'. She had already ransacked a full shelf of talcum powder and diarrhoea tablets and was heading towards the rail of luxury sanitary pads when a large figure approached her. She froze staring at the purple packaging.

"Hello Mar," said the busty bloke who towered over her.

"George!" cried Betty. She instantly relaxed and took hold of her trolley to steady herself.

"God, you've filled out a bit, since I last saw you."

George started blankly at his mother, his left eye wandering off in a new direction.

"God you stink of piss Mother!" George belched. Wiping away the stingy spit that dripped from his hairy chin he looked at his Mother, who was already staring with disgust at her only son.

"You vile pig! You're just like your father!"

Turning away she scratched her buttock then continued muttering wildly to herself. "Too bloody expensive anyway, only wanted them for me leakages."

As the pair continue their insults down the thinning street, they pass a jeweller's.

"Bloody Hell!" yelled Betty, as she stared in awe at

the glowing silver. George seemed too distracted with the crumpled betting slips, tobacco sleeves and empty pizza boxes that lay in the gutter to notice his plotting mother, who now had abandoned her trolley of stolen goods and had her nose pushed right up to the highly polished glass, as a security guard watched on from inside.

"Lord almighty! I want that necklace!" demanded a frantic Betty.

George finally looked at his mother, his huge belly hanging over his tight shorts. He sniggered. "And how are you going to pay for that mother? With Battenberg?"

He laughed pleased with his response, snorting through his large flared nostrils. There is an awkward silence, as a gentle wind blows through Betty's fine grey locks.

"I've got it George!" She slowly craned her neck towards her son, who was now rocking his heels against the curb. "We are going to steal the Jewels!" She squealed, choking in the excitement, gargling on cheese flavoured phlegm. "I have all the essentials; hip flask, joint cream, toothbrush and a clean pair of knickers." She looked delighted as she rubbed her hands together, grimacing at her reflection. "Now George, hit your mother as hard as you can!"

And before the last syllable had left poor old Betty's parched lips, George was raring up his fists. With George waiting cautiously outside, nibbling on a packet of salted crisps, Betty slowly hobbled into the jeweller's, her lip leaking blood.

"I've been mugged!" she dramatically wailed to the shocked assistants who all suddenly clambered towards her.

"Whisky, for the shock!" she whimpered, holding outstretched her shrivelled arm.

The male assistant rummaged in a panic in the loaded trolley, he threw pairs of gigantic knickers and Battenberg towards the wooden floor until he finally came across large bottles of whisky.

"Anyone for a tot of whisky?" asked Betty who was already feeling a little tipsy at the sight of the brown liquid. The smell of rejection filled Betty's nostrils, and from the look on her face she too wasn't sure if that smell was plain metaphorical or from her lack of hygiene, but a number of uneasy faces looked towards her.

"An old woman can't drink alone."

She sobbed, grabbing a stained tissue from her pocket to wipe her dry, unfazed eyes. Several minutes passed and after many poetic and saddening stories of decreased pets and crippling arthritis the staff had started handing out several glasses of Betty's counterfeit liquor and before long they too were weeping and collapsing into each other's arms unable to stand. Other members were clambering over the counter singing nursery rhymes and announcing lines of Shakespeare, so Betty moved towards the window of glowing silver, swiping the glistening platinum necklace encrusted with thousands of diamonds.

"Thank you very much!" A very drunk and disorientated Betty bowed as she staggered once again out of the jeweller's, several packets of Viagra falling down the left side of her stocking as she stumbled towards George who was fast asleep against a dustbin with a newspaper over his face.

"I'll be richer than the Beckhams!" she slurred, fisting the air in happiness.

So with the pair seeing pound signs they both took off into the darkened night, oblivious to the blue sirens that followed, and of course the tartan trolley was not too far behind them.

Even Dead Fish Float Down River

Melanie Rees

You'll get nowt but bloody dysentery from the Irwell, as few fish can survive the pollution and the heartache; the river suffocates under the weight of factory froth, stolen cars and misappropriated dreams.

Andi doesn't know why she thinks of fish or the river, maybe it's the way the nurse have positioned her legs on the hospital bed; knees propped over a pillow, her feet sort of bound together with a sheet to form a fish-tail. She feels the tug of cotton against her blackened ankles, her toes are cold but she waits.

There's only fifteen minutes left of visiting time. She waits.

She waits, only she doesn't even know if her mam is going to come, she hadn't even spoken to her. It was actually the ward sister who had rang her. Andi hadn't wanted to ring anyone, but the ward sister insisted the hospital had to contact somebody.

She knew they couldn't call him. He had been the one to drop her off at Accident and Emergency, 4.00 a.m. the night before. He hadn't even dampened the engine of his blue BMW, just leaned over and opened her door.

Before she got out, he had kissed her, the barracuda kiss of soft lips hooking together that she couldn't work out, where her mouth finished and his began.

They hadn't been able to come straight away after the 'accident', as he had to sober up first. "The police could pull me over, if I drink and drive... You wouldn't want me arrested, would you?"

It wasn't a direct threat, but the sing-song tone of his voice prophesised danger and she had read enough of

Greek literature to know this tone signified the circling of crows above the kitchen sink. They'd been together since she was sixteen, but it had taken her nearly two years to navigate the waterways of his moods. He wasn't a bad man; he even allowed her to go college once a week to do her 'A' levels. She worked in an office the other four days, but she was simply a drab shadow inside a cubicle at work, it was only in college she let herself wear the light.

It was college and her 'A' Level theatre studies tutor who'd told her "drama, is only really life, but scripted" and it's her tutor's voice she hears now, so she leans across to the bedside cabinet, takes the acceptance letter from RADA from her handbag from and writes on the back:

SCENE ONE. DAY. HOPE HOSPITAL

> ANDI *eighteen lies on a hospital bed. She is three months pregnant with a child which will not survive. She has a black eye and a bite mark above her left ear. The mark will leave a scar. Her mother enters, all coal black curls and French cigarettes.*

DAUGHTER: Mam, I need to ask you something?

MOTHER: Well, what you want?

DAUGHTER: I need to come home. Can I come home?

> *Silence*

MOTHER: Of course you can, Andi.

Lights

No, her mam would bark the three syllables beat of Andrea, never use her pet-name, would put up more a fight and Andi knew, despite the griping spasms in her abdomen, bubbles in her head, she had to stay true to her characters. She stares at the clock and thinks of fish.

FLASHBACK: PEEL PARK. AUTUMN 1982. DAY.

Two freckled sisters hold branches into the Irwell. The older sister has taken off her washing-machine dyed grey-white socks, tied them to the end of their branches, the sisters fish for tiddlers in the murky ink of the Irwell. The socks are filling with slime, debris and treasure. Their mother sits on a picnic blanket reading the Guardian newspaper, drinking a can of cider and fiddling with her nose ring. She does not yet have tattoos; those will come after the divorce.

LITTLE SISTER: Mam, Mam, we've caught a fish.

MOTHER: Don't be daft; you'll catch nowt but bloody dysentery in that muck… The fishes packed their suitcases a long time ago, nowt in there but Mr Rat and mind you don't wake him up or he'll have you for his bride.

They giggle, as little sister fishes out a rusty silver car key ring from her sock and holds it up to the Salford skyline. Big sister watches as little sister clenches her fingers around her silver fish and the blue pools of her face fill with slurry.

BIG SISTER: Don't listen to her? It is a fish, but its dead special, tropical even, probably swam upstream from Birmingham, maybe even London... best if we throw it back in so she can get where she needs to be. Come on; give it me, before Mam sees.

Little sister gives big sister the fish.

But before Andi can throw the car keyring back into the hub-capped teeth of the river, remember her and little sister smiling, suddenly the aroma of French cigarettes invades her nostrils and she senses a presence in the chair beside her bed.

The chair coughs, sharp like machine gun fire, Andi presses her eyelids tight together trying to remember her cough identification decoder; harsh and raspy means angry, a tickly cough means 'now', but what does sharp, repetitive cough mean? She can't think, her head feels like November.

The 'now' cough follows and she opens her eyes.

DAUGHTER: You've come?

MOTHER: Had to... Hospital rang me at seven this morning, bloody seven on a Sunday. It woke me and Marcel up... And we were out late at a do last night... can't stay long as he's got a gig tonight.

DAUGHTER: Sorry, they woke you... erm... thanks for coming.

MOTHER: Well, what do you want?

DAUGHTER: Can I?

MOTHER: No.

DAUGHTER: But Mam, I haven't even asked you...

MOTHER: No... you're not staying with me and that's final.

DAUGHTER: But it's only for a few months. I got this... I'm going to go to London in September. *Daughter shows her mother the RADA acceptance letter. The mother reads, her nicotine yellowed fingers soiling the pristine white of the paper.*

MOTHER: RADA? With a kiddie tied around your neck? Get real; you can't be dragging a kiddie halfway round the country. You made your bed; now lie in it...

DAUGHTER: But Mam...

MOTHER: But Mam, nowt. You can't have both. If anybody knows that, it's me. I'm thirty eight years old and spent most of my life raising kids. It's my time now... Do you hear that?... Will you, stop looking at me like that, I've got you the number of the women's refuge on Lower Broughton road. You know it; we stayed there when you were little. I've rang them and they are expecting you... here give us that pen.

64

Daughter hands mother the pen. Mother writes a telephone number down just above daughter's name on the letter, each press of the nib feels like a stab in her chest. Daughter pulls her feet apart, lets her legs thrash on the bed. Daughter struggles to breathe and a woman stage left begins to cry.

DAUGHTER:I know Mam, that's why…

MOTHER: Stop pulling your face, you can always apologise to him for whatever it is that you've done.

Silence

MOTHER: What did you do, anyway? If anyone knows what you're like, it's me…

DAUGHTER: I got into RADA, that's what I did.

MOTHER: Well, I'm not surprised he's pissed off. I bet you did it behind his back. How do expect to keep a fella, when you are running off here, there and everywhere?

DAUGHTER: Mam… it doesn't matter, visiting time is over… Bye

Silence

MOTHER: What were your audition piece, anyway?

DAUGHTER: *Taming of the Shrew* and Jo's monologue from *A Taste of Honey.*

65

Mother gives Daughter back the letter and then she laughs the throaty laugh she usually reserves for French men and bailiffs.

MOTHER: Well, *A Taste of Honey* is good training for young motherhood in Salford, I suppose?

DAUGHTER: Well, you'd know, wouldn't you...? I... I... Bye... *(Pause)* Mam.

MOTHER: Bye, Andrea.

Andi does not watch her mam leave the ward. She does not watch her hesitate like a new-born calf in the unfamiliar heels she's taken to wearing. She knows that even though her mam may wobble, she will hold her head higher than a TV aerial, arms folded across her chest, the walk all Salford women learn in school. The walk that betrays the gentleness of a thousand women waiting outside factory gates, contradicts the tears of the battered women and betrays the ripened smile Salford women hide inside, but warns instead "Fuck with me and you're for it."

She pulls the pillow from under her knees and puts it over her head, inhaling the fabric so she feels the familiar sensation of drowning. She splutters, lifts the pillow off for one, two, three... four seconds then pushes it back down hard until her eyes close and she fake sleeps until she hears the footsteps of the ward doctor the next morning.

He is all beard and good intentions; he takes her pulse so gently she has to blink away her rage.

"You said you tripped downstairs last night... maybe you can remember more now you've had a bit of sleep?"

She shakes her head and hides the truth inside the

66

bedsheets. She makes no eye contact with the doctor and after fifteen minutes of him asking questions to her unresponsive form, he signs her release papers and informs her she is free to leave.

Andi dresses quickly into her grey shift work dress, her obligatory multi-coloured Drama student cardigan pulls on green CND socks and Adidas trainers. She looks down and realises she looks a bit of an odd-bod, laughs at her strange ensemble for an Ordsall girl, but she folds her arms across her chest, holds her foggy head high and leaves the hospital, stepping into the comfort of torrential rain.

Even though she has money in her purse to pay for the bus, she walks instead.

She doesn't know where she's going. Its two miles north to the semi-detached house, where she lives with him and two miles west to the women's refuge. She decides to walk with the weather, follow the flow of the rain. She holds her finger up in the air, just like she had seen them do in films and walks with rain dripping down the back of her grey dress, wind painting her hair across her face.

She walks alongside the changing landscape of Eccles New Road in the direction of Lower Broughton Road. Andi walks slowly, stopping to rest on stone walls, where she lifts her chin, gulps in rainwater from a black sky. As the road dissolves from detached brick houses, into a 1950's Council estate with red-brick chimneys (whose lyrical poems have been stolen by gas fires) until it forms the silver-blue high-rise flats of Salford precinct, Andi begins to realise the river and these Salford streets have exchanged places.

The river Irwell is chockfull with rubbish, industrial waste pumped from factories long closed, old cars, abandoned washing machines and rumour has it, there's a three piece leather suite clearly visible from the top of Cromwell Bridge. She knows there will come a time when you can walk straight across the Irwell without getting your trainers wet. So the architects compensate for demise of rivers by building towers of water-blue and grey, lampposts that flicker the silver sheen of river froth and the streets no longer run straight but bend and curve like the contours of a stream. Andi is certain there would come a point when river rats would build their nests on the front steps of Salford town hall, all boundaries have blurred; poverty and disillusionment has dragged this town, like its people beneath the water line.

As if to confirm her concussed theory, she has to high-jump over a broken sewer puddle which has formed where two streets part company. She feels a twinge in her right shoulder blade, could swear she feels the trickle of blood between her legs; her grey dress clings to the tiny frame of body and nausea undulates through her body like the sharp tongue of a wave. Andi wants to go home but isn't entirely sure where home is. She looks around and finds herself at the corner of Lower Broughton road.

Through the drizzle she can see 'Kev's pet shop', where she and her friend bought a half a hamster each, when they were twelve. A hand-made sign in the window says 'Tropical Fish for only a pound" and she follows the lure of words inside.

A bell rings and Kev seems to remember her as she enters his shop door. Without saying anything he rushes into the back and fetches a towel. The pet shop smells of straw, dogs and familiarity. When they were twelve, her and her friend used to say Kev reminded them of a hamster. It was not meant as an unkind comparison but he is all beer-gut, ginger fur and cheeks that look like they were smuggling hornets.

He offers her a faded yellow towel with his right hand and in his left he cradles a can of 'Carling' which he takes furtive sips from in between conversation.

"What can I do you for, pet?"

"Oh ta for towel… I want a tropical fish for a pound, please"

Kev stares at her, his eyes narrowing so they seem to disappear in the swelling of his cheeks. Andi arranges the towel into a turban on her head while he takes a swig from his can. But it suddenly dawns on her, that it's her, who looks a right state, dripping wet, black eye and without a coat.

"You got a proper tank? I don't like to think of them going and being shoved in a little bowl. It's not right… not right… Ah, but you're a good girl, so I'll trust you with one of me fancy ones"

Andi nods her head and he puts his can down on top of a hamster cage and manoeuvres her gently to the aquarium. She allows herself to be moved by his huge hands and for the first time in two days her heart beat begins to calm.

"By god, girl, you're dripping… You'll catch your death of cold; you can borrow my brolly if you like? I'll go get in from back; you just go and see which fish you want."

The aquarium is a blur of colour and movement and she's not sure she will be able to choose just one fish, but then she spots a rainbow tailed fish hiding behind a wishing well.

Kev returns and Andi just gestures to the timid fish. "That's a guppy and a good choice for a first timer," Kev says as he pulls out a plastic carrier from his back pocket; half fills it with tank water and then grabs a neon fishing net from the side. Andi watches as he penetrates the waterline and begins to flood the net. There is a flurry of agitation but her fish just seems to swim towards captivity.

He pulls out the net and drops the fish into the plastic bag. There is something comforting about the way he twists the bag and ties the end with red plastic fastener. He hands her the bag and his old fishing umbrella, Andi gives him a pound and hands him back his towel.

She wants to say thank you, but she and the guppy are one, inside the plastic carrier, so she just offers him a ripened smile.

He seems to understand and pats the top of her still damp hair. She walks to the door, looks back at him and sees him shaking his head, swigging from the can. He sorts of lifts his hand in a non-committal wave and she closes the shop door.

Clutching the plastic bag, she walks across the road to Peel Park. The guppy thrashes in annoyance making the carrier bounce. "Well, you've changed your tune, haven't you? All meek and mild with your mates... don't worry. I'm taking you home."

This seems to soothe the temperamental guppy and they walk across the park in mutual silence. The grass bounces beneath the soles of Andi's trainers making her feel buoyant as she strides with purpose to the bridge that crosses to the university. She slip-stumbles down the embankment and the rain makes the bank a canvas so she can see her own small footprints following her in the mud.

She falls and the bank slaps her with its muddy hands, smearing her dress, but she holds the bag high above her head and slides on her bottom to the river's edge.

Standing with her toes over the edge she screams to the black sky "I'm not afraid of the darkness outside. It's the darkness inside houses I don't like" over and over and over again until her throat constricts and the only release she feels is when she unties the top of the plastic carrier and hurls the guppy to the open mouth of the river.

You'll get nowt but bloody dysentery from the Irwell, as few fish can survive the pollution and the heartache, the river suffocates under the weight of factory froth, stolen cars and misappropriated dreams.

But what of my fish, Andi sobs to nobody; it cannot articulate the pain of suffocation beneath an urban landscape. Somewhere in the dark place, just above her left ear, Andi knows what it is, the fish feels.

Suffocation feels like a semi-detached fist plunged into your spine at the top of the stairs or the gutting of a belly with the sharp blade of a 'you can't stay with me'. But, Andi smiles, as she throws the acceptance letter into the river, knowing, even dead fish float down river.

Fresh out the Pond

Alex James

My mate Tom is so top. He lives in Worsley an' me Mam
sez only gangsters an' footballers live there. I don't know
which one 'e is. We're only twelve and I don't fink you can
be a footballer or a gangster when you're twelve. I 'ave to
walk for fifteen minutes along the Bridgewater canal to get
to 'is 'owse. He's got a mobile phone but I an't got one.

We like to play in the woods on this walkway. We go
lookin' for newts. The Linear Walkway is dead long and
stretches under about three motorways. It starts at one end
of Salford an' ends at the other but I've never walked all
the way to either end. I'm not allowed to go that far. And
there's Kempnough Brook, which is, like, a little stream or
summat, and it runs next to the walkway through the
woods. In the spring there's these massive puddles that
gather just off the paff. They're, like, tempry ponds and
they grow algae on top an' you wun't fink anyfin' lives in
there but stuff does. Me and Tom go down wiv a bucket,
just in wellies and shorts, and we get newts, an'
sometimes little frogs, an' we put them in the bucket, and
we carry them to Tom's pond in 'is back garden. 'Is
garden is massive compared wiv ours.

We put the newts on the side, like, on the little patio
'round the water, relaxin' in the sun. And then we look a
couple of days later, to see if they've settled in, an' we can
never see a single one of them. Not one. Ever. Tom's Dad
always sez we've killed them.

"You din't mean to," he says, "but you've fed them to
the birds."

*Tom's got two sisters. They're older than us. One day
Emily, the youngest, got flashed on the Linear Walkway by*

72

*a man in an overcoat like the one Granddad used to wear.
Me Mam said it definitely wasn't Granddad though 'cos 'e
was dead by then. We weren't allowed to go down to the
woods for a bit but then Tom's Dad, who's dead high up
in the police, found the man an' put 'im in jail. I
remember being round at Tom's when his sister came
'ome. She was crying so 'ard that it looked like her eyes
would pop out. She kept runnin' out of breff 'fore she
could finish a sentence. She was doing the kind of bawlin'
I do when me Mam sez "stop cryin' or I'll give you
something to cry about!"*

Today we're goin' to the massive pond. Tom can't
remember where it is an' he's bein' dead mopey. I
remember it's the one be'ind the school footie pitch.
Tom's good wiv measurements and 'e said it's about four
metres wide an' five metres long. We don't know 'ow
deep it is 'cos we've only ever been in so the water comes
up just under our knees. Once I slipped a bit an' one of me
wellies filled up with water an' it stank for ages. We walk
through a row of tall trees near the corner flag an' it's
there – this weird, murky pool, surrounded by the junk o'
the woods. Bits of bark an' twigs an' ivy an' weeds
growing everywhere.

"What you bein' mopey for, Tom?"

"My Mum and Dad have had an argument."

"Should we not take the newts today? Bin wondering
if we should do it, anyhow. Like yer Dad sez, we've killed
a lot of newts."

"Or fed a lot of birds," Tom said.

We laugh.

"Come on."

He paddles into the water a bit.

"I only want hard newts from now on," Tom sez,
"ones that can fight off birds!"

I crouch down at the side of the pool and scan the surface for signs of life. A few water-flies an' skaters buzz about on top o' the water. There must be a footie game happ'nin on the field 'cos I can 'ear people shouting instructions to each uvver and booting the casey up and down. I try ta look through the murk an' see if there's any fish – sometimes you get sticklebacks or whatever flushed in off the stream. I can't see anyfin. I stand up an' wander back to the walkway. It's mad how quiet it is. Look left, look right – it's just paff an' trees for yards and yards into the distance. It's like the woods have swallowed us up.

Both Tom's sisters are beautiful. One of them has black hair and one of them has blonde hair. Everyone always teases Tom that they 'ave different Dads. Me Mam says the kids take the piss because they're jealous. Emily, the one who got flashed, is shorter and has blonde hair. Libby is tall and has dark hair. It's black like the end of a struck match. An' her hair is so long she has to twizzle it round her hand an' wrist for ages to tie it up. Libby's my favourite. I told me Mam once that I like her and me Mam said, "she'd eat you for breakfast."

Tom loses 'is balance and kind of sploshes furver into the bog. He disturbs all the algae an' makes breaks in the emerald foam. The water is brown with earth an' dirt an' foliage. I move round to the far side o' the pool where the ground is soft an' boggy. I search for movement.

"Nothing here is there mate?"

"Maybe sack it off today," I say.

Tom runs his 'and through the water like a capsized shark fin.

"You're not going home?" says Tom.

"Might" I said.

"I don't wanna go home."

"Why? Have you bin done for summat?"

74

"The police are round."

And Tom looked dead small, stood there up to 'is shins in the pond, like a water feature. I could tell he was scared.

"The police are always round yours."

"This lot aren't Dad's mates. They're… different. They're from another station. I know 'cos my Mum had a panic when they came in."

You can nip through the woods as a shortcut to our school. Tom said Emily won't come the Linear Walkway anymore. I don't get why 'cos the perve who showed 'is willy to 'er is locked up now. I s'pose she just remembers it whenever she finks about the paff or the woods or how quiet it is. Now she gets the bus to school. Libby still walks.

I pick up a thin stick an' move some floating leaves to one side. I don't know what to say. Tom's just stood there starin' into the muck. I steal quick looks at 'im but I'm still scanning to see if there's anything of interest in the water. Someone scores in the footie game 'cos there's cheering an' then swearing and I hear the keeper go "where's the flippin' defence?" Tom changes the subject.

"Do you reckon you'd die if you swam in there?"

"No but you'd smell for ages."

"You can test it then, you've got nothing to lose!"

"Piss off."

"Dad says that when it goes stagnant you can get a rash and a tummy bug and all sorts."

"Stagnant?"

"When it goes off and dries up, in the middle of summer."

Tom runs both hands through the water.

"Dare me to swim a length?"

"We don't know how deep it is."

"You'll have to be a lifeguard if I start drowning."

I've never told Tom that I can't really swim.

I see this newt sprint out from under a lily leaf. Its little legs are clogged wiv mud but it darts for the water determinedly.

"There's one!" I shout.

But Tom's already half belly-floppin' into the water. He goes in almost face first an' makes a giant splash. A bird flaps an' scrambles off through the branches into the sky above the woods. Tom stands up an' shakes out his arms. He's covered in scraps of shrubs an' looks like a monster coming out of a swamp – spurting water out of his mouth an' spitting out bits of algae. He scoops up some wet mud from the verge and smears it on his face.

"Bleurghhhh, I'm a swamp monster!"

He's wades in a bit deeper, nearly up to his waist. He's laughing at first, and I'm laughing, but then he freezes.

"Something just touched my leg."

"What, something moving?"

Tom starts to edge out of the water, boggy mud squelching under his weight. I can see something bobbing just under the surface. Like, moving in slow motion. In an' out of the shadow of the muck and the overhangin' trees.

"It was… hard and cold."

Tom's shakin' a bit now. He's wrapped his arms around himself and he's stood looking into the water, spooked.

"Someone's probably dumped a shopping trolley in there."

I squat down and I can see a… shape… just below the surface of the pool. It's a grey colour, sort of. It looks weird 'cos it's such a different colour to everything. I move some of the muck around and I can see there's, like, a vine of ivy wrapped up with this shape. All 'round us it's the shade of the wood – brown an' green – and this thing it's, like, well it's like it doesn't even have a colour.

"Let's go." Tom says, and I can tell he's freaked out.

I folla the length of the vine with me stick an' I grab the end that's juttin' out of the water, restin' on the bank. I pull on it a bit an' I'm pullin' against a heavy weight for a second, then it snaps. I'm stood there with it in my hand. We're both frozen staring, dripping wet, fixed on it. Our eyes follow the stringy, sinewy green length down to the end nearest the water – it's like a tentacle I've just ripped from a sea creature.

At the end of the vine, wrapped tightly like string, there's a knot of hair – a knot of pitch-black hair.

Tom starts to cry.

The Trajectory of Patrick Brown

Zoe Lambert

There has been a trajectory in Patrick Brown's life, which has led inexorably to the moment he finds himself lying on a bleach-smelling floor of Salford Royal, staring up at the grey cracked ceiling of a theatre in urology. He blinks at a nurse, who is saying, "Are you OK, sir, can you hear me?" His wife, Frankie, calling his name from the operating table where the consultant stands over her, announcing, "I've done it! I've got the damn thing in!"

As he lies on the floor, he can see the flashes in his trajectory, a trajectory he'd assumed was aligned with Hegel's notion of thesis, antithesis and synthesis, a notion of history moving in tiny steps towards a better world. He had never seen himself as having a large role to play; he was no Trotsky, no Luxembourg, no Che Guevara. He was rank and file. What mattered was the daily work: the meetings, supporting *The Morning Star* and every damn strike and union action. From the poll tax in the eighties to NHS privatisation and the cuts, he was there with his home-made banners, a T-shirt for every campaign.

Amidst the cracks in the ceiling, he sees the first stage in his trajectory: the fact he was shopping in B&Q when the Berlin Wall fell. Married for five years, Frankie pregnant with Polly, he was then teaching history at Buile Hill High. He'd once said loudly in a pub that the rise of B&Q was the rise of bourgeois DIY, stealing labour from skilled working class artisans. But when they moved into their own creaky house in Eccles, Frankie was disappointed he couldn't put up a shelf. On the 9th of November, he found himself driving to B&Q after school. He asked the security men in the entrance lodge for directions to the rawl plugs but they were watching the Six O'clock news on a small TV: images of East Berliners heading to the West in cars and on foot. He'd had to sit down on one of the chairs, his head in his hands while the security men tried to guess how high the wall was, and whether they'd be able to climb it. The next day, he'd gone to the *Morning Star* for insight, their headline confirming: 'GDR Unveils Reform Package.'

The second development was his family's slip into consumerism. Though he'd first met Frankie at a CPGB meeting in Moss Side in 1979, she had, with two children and an inexplicable fatigue, gradually let her membership slip. 'I'm too tired,' she'd say before meetings. "I'm staying home. You go."

His lovely, vivacious, take-no-nonsense Frankie spent more and more time in bed, with little Polly and Simon standing at the door, saying, "What's wrong with Mummy?"

"Mummy's poorly today."

Years of taking his kids to Manchester Museum to see the snakes and dinosaur bones so 'Mummy can have a rest', of holidays where she stayed in the caravan while they went for hikes, of Frankie being reprimanded by the catering manager for 'too many sick days', until one day Frankie told Patrick she had an appointment with the neurologist.

While Polly came home with bags of cheap, disposable Primark clothing, and flatly refused to join the Young Communist League: "What dad? There's like three of them." Frankie started watching QVC after her primary school made her redundant: "We've made all the legal concessions and alterations we can for a catering assistant. There is a point when employees just have to come to work." So instead of serving lunch to children, she bought

OPI nail varnish, "Such lovely colours, Patrick," and Yankee Candles and SBC Arnica Gel, "It eases the tightness in my legs, see," and a myriad of unidentifiable creams and lotions.

The next stage in his decline had been when he walked into his son's bedroom, to find fifteen-year-old Simon reading Ayn Rand's *Atlas Shrugged*.

So Patrick sat down on the bed, and had a frank discussion about what he termed a 'cult', and his son had revealed that he:

A) no longer believed in socialism as a viable alternative

B) thought Ann Rand was talking sense

C) wanted to work for Shell.

During these revelations, Simon had not moved from his single bed, where he had been lying on his front reading. Patrick staggered backwards, shaking his head and saying, "Where did I go so wrong?" It was not his way to enforce things on his children. He preferred to reason, but even so, he'd shouted: "Libertarianism is the philosophy of teenagers. It's pure selfishness," and stormed out of the room.

With Frankie unable to climb the stairs, she had to move into the living room. They got rid of his desk and a bookcase to make room for the wheelchair and bed from social services. When he pressed a button, the bed went up and down.

"It just seems wrong," he said. "You down here and me upstairs."

"I know, but what can we do? There's no room for two beds in here."

Some mornings, he struggled to get her up and into a chair before he left for school, so she stayed in bed till he got home. But they managed, just Frankie and him, with the kids at school and university; busy with their own lives.

One morning, he peered under the bed, looking for a lost sock, when he found a stack of QVC boxes hidden beneath it. Frankie was watching a woman selling imitation Jacqueline Kennedy jewellery on the QVC flatscreen TV.

"How did these get here?" he asked.

"Oh, the delivery lady brings them in. She's so kind."

He tried hard not to sound accusing. "I'm a bit worried about your spending. There's only my wage now. You haven't even got DLA or PIP or whatever it is. How are you paying for all this?"

"You just don't understand, do you?" she said. "You just don't understand anything other than your bloody strikes."

There were times when Patrick sat in an NUT meeting, trying to keep his eyes open from tiredness, his back aching from lifting his wife, when he'd start to wonder at his trajectory, at how with the downstairs bed he couldn't climb in and kiss her; how, when he tried to touch her she said, "That hurts." But he rallied himself to get on with the job with Stackovian spirit. He'd begun thinking about the conditions of care as work, work which is unvalued and unpaid. When he told Frankie, she got that wearied look, that here-we-go-again look, but writing an article about the economic role of carers for *The Morning Star* was a boost. Polly phoned from university when she read it: "Dad, it's like you got your mojo back." Other carers emailed him to share their experiences, and he started a campaign with the TUC for flexible hours.

"What is this about you?" Frankie asked, one evening when he got home from school. "You're always taking over everything; turning it into one of your campaigns. Why can't you leave things alone?"

Then, as the nurses got her ready for the procedure, she looked at him. "Thank you for coming," she said, lifting her hand to touch his cheek. "You were at both births too, making a nuisance of yourself, pestering the midwives about joining a union."

He laughed. Yes, he had certainly annoyed them.

But in the operating theatre, as he stood and peered over the barrier, he'd seen what they had done to his beautiful Frankie, still so lovely, still so kind, lying on a table, with a tube coming out of her, and a cowboy consultant shouting, "Bingo!"

In this moment, as he sinks to the floor, he realises, with the ceiling swimming above him, that he has been wrong all his life; he is not a small but meaningful part of the greater sweep of history; he is not an element of the synthesis after all. No. Instead, he is nothing but a speck in the universe, and the universe is not moving forwards, it is imploding, and he is just a swirling particle in the chaos.

Murray Mints

RBN Bookmark

The world passed me by as I watched idly on.

Staying true to the advert, I was letting the train take the strain.

The grimy window I gazed thru had not it seemed, been graced by a window cleaners shammy since the age of steam. I could almost picture Tony Robinson and the Timewatch team conducting an archeological dig on the window pane.

On the table opposite of me was an unfurled copy of The Times newspaper, beside it lay an open tartan spectacle case. In its confines, a neatly folded cleaning cloth tucked away neatly in the bottom half. I tried hard to guess the various colours in the tartan pattern, but to no avail. My colour blindness reigned supreme yet again.

The owner of these items was a rotund gentleman, his brown turtle shell spectacles had slipped half-way down his nose, had he opened his mouth he would have undoubtedly swallowed them in a single gulp. He sat embedded into his seat, his eyes at half-mast.

His look was one of a constipated Buddha with a lot on his mind.

He was obviously a London city gent, around 45 years old at a guess, stockbroker or something along those lines.

The look of distain about him when I stepped onto the train and occupied the window seat opposite him did not go unnoticed.

We made eye contact, I nodded.

He didn`t.

We didn´t speak… how could we?

The trip home from Peterborough that sunny August

day in 1983 was devoid of social niceties.

On occasion when the trolley lady would wheel her wares along the aisles, I would buy a bag of cheese and onion crisps along with a can of Fosters lager. The sound of me devastating those tasty Golden Wonders only deepened the chasm between the city gent and me.

I didn`t sleep on the journey home to Manchester, and the plentiful amount of noise pollution I served up, ensured my table company didn`t either.

"Next stop Manchester," came a female voice over the tannoy system.

I opened my mouth and emptied the few remaining crisps down my gullet, and then neatly folded the empty crisp bags, before inserting them into the three empty Foster`s cans I had lined up in front of me.

As the train pulled into Manchester`s Piccadilly station, I stood up and removed my holdall from the luggage rack above my head.

The city gent was in nap mode, now that I was all crisped and lagered out.

He slept, oblivious to my departure.

His newspaper, now thinly covered in crisp droppings that had mysteriously made their way over from my side of the table. The only visible sign our paths had ever crossed.

A sign of The Times I thought to myself, before exiting the train.

It`s nice to come home but the euphoria soon wears off, a bit like sex really. The only difference being one doesn`t have to take a shower afterwards.

Once outside I could see it was raining in true Manchester style. It was late evening, a typical grey day in the North West of England, aye it`s grim up North so they say.

I made my way from the train station, taking a shortcut to Chorlton St Bus Station and was shortly greeted by a woman's voice.

"Hello love, you looking for business?" she asked.

Absence might make the heart grow fonder but it also makes one quite forgetful, the proof being I had forgotten Chorlton Street was a notorious red light district back then.

"Sorry love but I'm gay. Can't you see the damp patch on the seat of my trousers?" I replied tongue in cheek.

She looked at me a bit, well queer I suppose, before shrugging her shoulders and resuming her search for a punter elsewhere.

Having run the gauntlet of Chorlton Street, my damp patch and I crossed Portland Street and made our way to Piccadilly Bus Station. It was Friday evening and some of the weekend revelers had started early, my bus stop was easy to see. Some kind soul had denoted it with a crusty pizza sized vomit which was still emitting steam.

The number 82 bus arrived on time and I sat downstairs with the old ladies rather than go upstairs and face the high-spirited rowdies who had piled onto the bus without paying.

A kindly old lady saw my bag and asked me if I had been on holiday.

I replied that I'd been working down South and I was only back home visiting relatives for the Bank Holiday.

"I was down South once. It was when my husband was still here mind," she said.

"I am sorry, has he been dead long?" I asked.

"Dead, good god no but if I ever catch up with him and that trollop he ran off with then he'll wish he was," she said with a murderous twinkle in her eye.

I offered her a Murray Mint as we sat and chatted

about everything under the sun, not that solar activity was particularly evident in that day in Manchester.

She said how much she enjoyed our chat and wished me luck, I thanked her and wished her the same, and her ex-husband even more should she ever catch up with him, before getting off the bus on Alexandra Road in Moss Side.

As I walked up the driveway to my parent's house, memories from the past came flooding back. I recalled how difficult it was when I left home, I could never imagine it would feel just as difficult returning again.

I could hear my parent's dog barking and then caught sight of his face at the door, as he brushed aside the lace curtains so as to see who was coming. The door swung open, releasing him as one would a greyhound from his starting box.

Mum's joy at seeing her son's return, telling me to dump my bag in the hallway, sit down and have a cup of tea and some fig rolls. Dad asking me how I was getting on down South, while keeping me up to speed on the comings and goings at Old Trafford.

The dog was hiding under the table, sat beside my feet, staring up at me with those sad dog eyes, hoping I'd feed him a biscuit.

Memories are a bit like a box of chocolates. We tend to pick and choose the ones we like best.

My Murray Mints spare me the hassle of choice. It's easiest that way.

One More Cup of Sugar

Angela Elizabeth Armstrong

Thursday 3:42pm. The familiar tap, tap, tap, TAP on the letterbox of number 63 indicated the presence of Shirley and her chipped coronation cup. Ada knew immediately of course who was summoning her. The rattle of the letterbox in this way was customary and she was well as acquainted with it. As acquainted with it as she was with the words which would inevitably follow on opening her door. "Can I borrow a cup of sugar Mrs P?" The fact that Shirley from next door but one always addressed Ada in this manner irritated her somewhat. Ada was a stickler for convention and although she had known Shirley as a neighbour for the best part of eleven years now, the fact that she was significantly older than her should inevitably command a degree of respect and formality rather than abbreviation. *She should say "May I borrow a cup of sugar?"* Ada mused silently. More to the point, Ada also knew that borrowing something usually called for giving that something back as a matter of courtesy. Ada never considered herself to be particularly academically inclined – that was a man's place in life – but she did understand and had a reasonable command of the English language. Whereas a book or an article of clothing would be easy enough to return, perhaps sugar was a different matter altogether Ada hypothesised. She didn't much mind though and hoped she was considered a good neighbour for her kindly and regular unreturned deed. It would seem too impolite, even a hostile gesture to ask for sugar of all things to be reimbursed.

Ah the sugar tap, Ada mouthed as she eased herself up from her chair where she had been resting for some time now due to feeling a little under the weather today. She walked automatically upon hearing the summons over to the kitchenette in the small back room. Stretching up slowly to retrieve the crumpled bag of white granules she eyed the sticky marks around the cupboard door handle as she opened it "Must give that a once over with a wet cloth," she whispered with conviction. In truth, Ada recognised she had promised herself on other occasions to clean it but hadn't got round to it yet on account of the all the aches and pains in her arms and other places these days. Approaching the front door, Ada contemplated why it was always sugar Shirley ran out of. This appeared to occur with the same frequency as the partially horizontal northern rain that was falling again outdoors. *Oh never in need of bread was Shirley, nor porridge oats or boot polish for that matter, the very staples of Salford life,...* "ALWAYS BLOOMIN' SUGAR!!" caught herself speaking aloud rather vociferously. The fact was, Ada didn't care much for sugar herself and considered it mostly unnecessary for day to day living. She really only bought sugar 'just in case'. Just in case of a visitor, just in case she fancied baking a cake (which she never did). Just in case, really. The events in her life had made Ada quite disparaging and sour, as sour as the sugar was sweet. She didn't quite know where this unresolved, virulent, unpleasantness should be directed anymore, but she was familiar with how she felt most days. A far cry from the vibrant, spirited, auburn-haired girl she had once been when she was still living at home and enjoying happy times with her kith and kin. How lively she was then with half a crown in her pocket, her hopes in her head and her dreams in her heart. Some admirers had said that she was pretty. She could have married a few chaps in the area but there was really only the one for her, Sweethearts they had been, cut from the same type of cloth and as happy together as the day was long. A far contrast to her present circumstances in life. Her very existence had taken its toll on her in the years that had passed.

"Can I borrow a cup of sugar Mrs P?" Shirley's commentary began before door had fully opened just as the coronation cup was plunged forward towards Ada's hand. Ada put on her best smile, *Pity you don't have occasion to use it more often* her inner voice taunted silently. It was now mostly reserved for her neighbour along with Mrs Worth at the corner shop and the odd random relative who may call if they happened to be passing by during the lead up to Christmas. Shirley gave the usual explanation, in her usual way, "It's for Jim you know." *It always is!* Ada's terse, cloaked, response came rapidly as her neighbour proceeded to launch into this week's latest gossip. This was usually the point Ada allowed her mind to contemplate better pursuits. If there was one thing she couldn't abide it was gossip and especially the second hand sort which Shirley Benson excelled in and usually involved the frequenters of those damnable hostelries on Broad Street or the trivial goings on of family life. *Alcohol and gossip... what a waste of anyone's time with a sufficient brain and the desire to use it wisely!!* If there was one thing Ada couldn't abide it was folk who did nowt constructive with their time when they were of an age and ability to do so. Actually, there were quite a few things Ada couldn't or wouldn't tolerate but she was a God fearing woman and lived her life according to what she felt right and just. She would always offer a helping hand to the afflicted or needy considering it her duty to do so even if the gesture wasn't returned! Deep down, she was really a bit of a soft touch but the depth of her convictions tended to fluctuate just that bit more now and the softer side wasn't always that discernible to those who didn't know her well. Ada forced herself to focus now being taken off guard by the strength of her beliefs. "…so that was that with our Jean and I told her so, more going on thirty five than thirteen that girl of mine… anyway, thanks again, must dash Mrs P." Ada knew not what had occurred with Jean and was bothered even less as she was brought abruptly and consciously back to her doorstep just as the remains of the crumpled sugar bag were placed back in her grasp. Shirley's easy going, grateful tap on Ada's withered hand acknowledged her neighbours kindness more than the older of the women knew. Ada barely had time to utter "Bye then" as Shirley was already back at her dwelling whose front door had been left open judging by the volume of Jim's voice bellowing at one or more of their off spring.

"How predictable that Shirley Benson is" Ada muttered as she bolted the sturdy door dislodging a small, unnoticed piece of flaky red paint. She didn't expect to see sight nor sound of anyone else today so the task was done and would save her a job before bed time. "Never one to suffer fools gladly our Ada" her sister had said to her more than once when they young women. The memory unexpectedly entered her head. However, Ada recognised that she didn't mind Shirley really, quite warmed to her in fact, despite her ramblings. Ada knew Shirley's life wasn't all a bed of roses like her own, what with five children and summat up with one of them at that not to mention a workshy husband who was unprincipled even when work was plentiful. Jim Benson liked to proclaim that he was 'limited' in what he could do on account of a mysterious injury he evidently sustained during his national service and which no one quite knew the character of. This was very much up for debate in Ada's mind. He was most unlike her own Harry. *He was a worker* and Ada held that thought proudly. For thirty one years thereabouts, she had watched him every morning as he put on his collar and tie before she adjusted his Windsor knot knowing it would provoke a loving smile on Harry's face and a peck on her cheek by way of a reward for her endeavours. Harry had done very well to gain and hold onto an office job at the local corporation office. He'd even had the odd promotion but circumstances put paid to his innate potential and further progression. He was a grammar school boy and rightly deserved his position in life. He'd come from a decent family, like herself and a strong work ethic had been the norm. Ada had relished this daily task as the happily married woman she once was. She desired in her mind's eye to adjust Harry's ties again but, he was long departed and only the memories stood robustly nowadays. They had been the type of couple who needed little more in life than the other, content just being together even when there was nothing much else to do. Occasionally, Ada would catch herself stroking his last good suit which she had kept all this time in the wardrobe they once shared as newlyweds. Money was a bit tighter then and both were of the 'make do and mend' persuasion though not frugal. The act of touching the cloth gave Ada momentary pleasure and it took her elsewhere. There had been a child, just the one, a boy they'd named Peter Harold. A bright, wonderful, freckle cheeked boy! Tragically, Peter's life ended brusquely when he seven years and fifty nine days old. The coal man's usually placid horse 'Yorkie Lad' was the perpetrator. Michael Taylor, the coalies apprentice, would tell people that Yorkie Lad had been given his name on account of the animal being born *ont' uther side of The Pennines*. Michael being the sort of lad that would have expected Yorkshire to be just as far away as Paris in his own world. Yorkie Lad had somehow broken free from the cart he had been pulling that day and had become severely startled by who knows what. The horse had ran wildly down the street where Peter had been playing and knocked him out of this world as well as ending the life of Mr Haig's display of fruit and vegetables outside his greengrocers shop around the corner. The horse itself died at a great age. How Ada would have flogged that particular dead horse given half the chance! At the time of Peter's death, there had been shock and grief and plenty of both. Ada never recovered. She never understood why she was expected to recover. The death of a child was not an illness that could be recovered from. She knew also that the luckless occurrence had brought about a change in Harry and ended his own life prematurely. Ada now kept them both in her heart and soul where nothing or no one could hurt either of them anymore. There had been a lot of gossip of course... oh the gossip! Ada and Harry managed their lives as best they could afterwards but they were private people essentially and well-meaning kindness from neighbours did little to bring sustained relief. If she'd heard the phrase "Oh he was a lovely boy Ada," anymore at the time she would have exploded outwardly. "Was". Past tense. Gone. Done. Finished. Words to denote an existence. Ada had always been one to live in the here and now and relished her life, but the tragic, overwhelming event put paid to that. The sole consolation was Harry was still around then to offer his usual style of comfort which though small in gesture came from a benevolent but shattered heart. Ada recognised the change in herself also in the weeks after Peter's death which had carried on to the present day etching his permanence on her demeanour. Shirley Benson droning on about her second youngest son's autism on occasions when sugar was called for didn't help. In truth, Ada didn't quite understand what autism was and neither did Shirley. There hadn't been such afflictions in her day. All she knew was that if she had a son with autism, she wouldn't be complaining about it. Just having a son in any shape or form would be a blessing enough.

4:01pm Ada settled back into the familiarity of her winged armed chair, which had been worn by the years as was her own body and both the chair and Ada suited one another. It had been an unusual gift from a maiden aunt who lived out her days on th' Height on the occasion of her marriage to Harry. She and Harry were intending to flit to Irlams o' th' Height themselves which would have been more suited to their circumstances with Harry having a good job and all. Peter had come along though and despite looking at a few garden terrace houses, the timing never seemed quite right after that so they remained just off Ellor Street, Hanky Park way, and did so contentedly being proud to fully own their little house. As she adjusted herself into the chair, its high back protected Ada in more ways than one but mostly from the draught which stealthily crept in through the sash window of the front room. She immersed herself into her copy of her favourite women's magazine which had landed on her coconut matting a while before. She pondered a while on this week's knitting pattern for a bolero in a particularly puce shade of yellow. Ada didn't care for it much but the pages of the magazine were generally a good read and a weekly treat she allowed herself. Mr O'Reilly the newsagent took his post seriously and it never failed to drop through the letterbox every Thursday afternoon. Daniel O'Reilly delivered it himself to Ada's house considering it necessity to do so. Ada was grateful for it. It was her main means of escapism these days.

93

6:42pm. Ada was awoken from her slumber rather abruptly by the raucous racket of Edna Bickershaw's laughter as she passed by the window. The magazine slid to the floor and stayed there as Ada craned her head to peer into the dimness outside. Edna Bickershaw, the most flamboyant personality in the neighbourhood! Edna could only be described as a larger than life character with a laugh and a hairdo to match. *One of the first women to have a blue rinse was Edna,* Ada recalled to herself. This had caused quite a stir at the time and Edna quite relished being a local celebrity for a week or so. Ada always thought Edna should own a name which was more suited to her presentation… Lavinia Lamour or Augusta Hepburn perhaps. Ada caught herself chuckling audibly and rather enjoyed the spontaneity of this and the feeling it gave her. She wished she could laugh more often these days but there was seldom the occasion to make the effort somehow. Her mind drifted. There wasn't much call in this day and age for names like 'Edna' or 'Bickershaw' or even her own. The world was progressing now and names were too. Only last week in her magazine Ada had heard of a woman in Suffolk who owned a double barrelled surname naming her baby daughter 'Tracey'. *My, how things are bloomin' changing* considered Ada when she had first read the tale.

6:51pm "Ah well, time for tea I suppose." Ada tottered to the back kitchen, down the worn step. Her hands struggled to open the small tin of red salmon advertising 6d off on the label. The meagre tin was her customary tea on a Thursday evening and usually eaten following her first thumb through of her magazine such was Ada's obligatory routine. It somehow added to a sense of occasion having two treats in one day, the magazine and salmon. "A slice of brown bread with best butter…" she said aloud "Just the one," as she busied herself a while. Her appetite was small nowadays like her body and one slice would be perfectly adequate and definitely satisfactory.

11:04 p.m. Ada was restless in her bed and in discomfort with what she supposed was indigestion and put this down to having her cocoa too late or the salmon being off. She only wished she could nod off now and get properly warm. She always hoped to dream of better days, days with Harry and Peter. Occasionally Ada did dream of them and this offered small solace. Peter was always wearing the V neck sweater she had lovingly made for him in his first year at school which he looked smashing in. How she longed to see her boys again.

Sunday 2:16pm. Shirley lifted the letterbox once more... tap, tap, tap, TAP... tap, tap, tap, TAP... TAP,TAP,TAP!!! "Mrs P... it's Shirley... are you there?" The coronation cup shattered into pieces as Shirley misplaced the position of the front step as she reached down without looking to place it there intending to look through the front bay window. Unceremoniously, the Queen's head parted company from her shoulders and Shirley for some reason fleetingly recalled Ann Boleyn's head doing the same sort of thing as she picked up what was left placing the fragments into her apron pocket. "Damn it, me best cup an' all."

Ada was sleeping contentedly and resting peacefully now... a safe and secure sleep at last. The merest hint of a smile was evident on her pale, frail lips. Her eyes softly closed.

Shirley went back inside number sixty one to fetch another receptacle in which the borrowed sugar could be poured. Mumbling to herself she was somehow feeling a little uneasy. What she didn't realise yet is that there

would be no more cups of sugar so readily available today
or ever... at least not from Mrs Ada Percival at number
63.

Retrospective

Ceila

"Actually, Salford is a really beautiful place; except most of the time you don't notice because it's either raining or you're getting mugged."

They were walking back from Salford Shopping City. It was a cloudy November day. Freezing cold.

Emma liked walking. She liked being outside. Dani didn't. She hated the underground passages beneath the streets they passed through to get to Tesco. Every time she walked under them, stories popped in her head of people who would drink themselves to death there, or gangs that used the dirty underground tubes for drug dealing. Her younger sister, on the other hand, would always make stupid cries and laugh at the echo of her own voice. Dani would count the leftover condoms at the sides of the tubes.

"Let's walk along the river today!" Emma said.

"It's not like there is another way..." Dani answered without taking her eyes away from her phone.

They came out of the underground passages in Cromwell Rad and Emma took the turn next to the towering Anglican Church. In the far end of the yard, behind the church's fence, there were two gravestones. They stood apart from the others; lonely, yet together in eternity. Emma thought of them to have been a couple, and she would make stories of how the lovers had met, or what had happened to them.

"Do you think these two were married Dani?"

"It's a war memorial! For fuck's sake Emma..." her sister replied and turned her attention back in her phone.

Emma looked at the church. She thought it was beautiful because of the large grass yard that surrounded it. She wished her family would attend the mass on Sundays, and then have a walk or go for tea.

Why it is that Salford has this reputation, she wondered. *After all, the entirety of England is grey and rainy. Is it because Manchester's working class misfits were somehow all exiled here? Who knows...* It is what it is. And now it won't change.

You see, Salford is the perfect place for adolescent crime stories. Teenagers getting in fights, having their formative trouble with the law, forming gangs and finding excuses to fight, all of that so they can forget the real reason for their distress. That's what Dani had told her before she went to college. Now that she had become a freshman she rarely spend any time with Emma, or her family for that matter.

"Dani, why does Salford have this reputation?"

"Haven't you noticed that not a lot of people move in Salford?" Her eyes were still on the screen.

"But why?"

"'There are lucky ones who get out, but most residents have settled here for generations, and simply can't get away. Be it teenage pregnancy, parents drawing kids into their jobs, not high enough GCSEs... For whatever reason, they got stuck here."

Dani was only sixteen, but she was old enough to understand the difference between Salford and the rest of the world. She liked watching TV. When she was growing up, she had to babysit Emma all the time. Without her parents around, she was free to cuddle in the couch and watch TV until hearing the car pull outside sometime past midnight. In the mornings, she saw her mates fight behind the school alleys, the college kids shagging in the girls' bathroom, her classmates smoking cigarettes in between breaks and eventually upgrading to pot. In the evenings she preferred to see New York, Paris, London, Italy, South America, New Orleans, Los Angeles... All she knew was everywhere else would be better than here. The grass is greener, especially when it barely grows in Salford.

"Be real for a moment," she said to Emma. "If you had the chance, would you get out of here?"

Emma was silent. She didn't understand what her sister was trying to get to.

"Would you?" she asked back.

"Yes!" Dani exclaimed as if it went without saying.

That's it. People simply wanted to get the fuck out. Don't swear... Emma tried to get her thoughts in order. She wanted to understand Dani. She turned her head down looking at her worn brown boots. Her sister turned her attention back to typing.

Dani knew there was nowhere else to look besides her phone. They'd left behind Castle Irwell and were heading down Seaford Road, past the same looking streets with same looking houses, same looking pavements and same looking shops. The past few years, there had been so many constructions in Salford. Chapel Street had been reconstructed, new University buildings were built, new apartments, the MediaCity development... It was as if they wanted to tear down Salford's infamous reputation along with the old buildings. For an outsider, it would be easy to think of Salford as a restless place. But Dani knew that it only took a short walk from all these new constructions to get to see the real Salford. Old, crumbling, neglected houses, dirty streets and a festering culture. Even the language did not sound the same anymore...

They kept walking silently. Emma was observing the houses. Some had chimneys, some had front gardens, some had colourful windows or decorated doorbells. They had passed a house build at the foreground of the meadows, which looked like it came straight out of the Hansel and Gretel fairy-tale; except it had no candy roof. They slowly left the buildings behind and came to the football fields. It was as if they had suddenly been cut off from the noisy town and entered a world consisting only of tall grass and trees.

Would I ever come back here? Dani wondered. She looked around. Her sister was walking ahead with her head peaking at all little details of the scenery around her. She tried hard to remember whether there was anything she liked about Salford as a child. *The world must seem so different when you're a kid,* she thought. *Everything looks taller, and prettier...*

For a moment, she wished she was still a kid. She put her phone in her pocket.

They crossed the green bridge at River Irwell. She saw a swan. Maybe the river was not just a mosquito and spider retreat. Yes, it was immensely dirty, and smelly and not at all romantic! But there were the football fields around it, and Peel Park with the playground. The grass in Peel Park is evergreen, so it grows all year around, except maybe for the winter when it is covered in snow. She used to go there when she was little with all her friends, and they had snow-fights until they would freeze!

Was Salford a question of perspective? Or had she only seen its ugly face.

"Dani, is that a man?"

Emma brought her out of her contemplation. They were now crossing the red and white bridge above the second canal of the river.

"Are you seeing ghosts Emma?"

"No, look, there is a man there under the bridge! He is reaching for something in the water!"

Dani looked closer. Somehow, a piece of fabric had ended on top of the rocks at the side of the river. With a bit of imagination, it looked like a homeless man wrapped in a cape who was bending over something above the riverside. In reality, it was a stranded piece of old fabric hanging in the rocks.

She laughed at her sister.

"It's a rag, Emma! You kids are crazy!"

Emma pouted. She didn't like feeling stupid. Dani noticed her.

"Do you wanna know something funny?" she asked her.

"Yes!" Emma exclaimed.

"Did you know that cab drivers are obligated to carry hay at all times?"

"What?"

"Cab drivers are obliged by law to carry hay. In their trunk."

Emma stared at her.

"Why?"

"It's one of these bullshit British laws which has never been repealed."

"Why would cab drivers be associated with hay in the first place?"

"It dates back to... I don't know, the 1800's? You know, when cabs were not cars but horse carriages. So I guess they need to have hay in the truck so they could feed the horses in case they got hungry."

They started laughing. The afternoon light was fading, and it was getting misty. Dani heard the waterfalls at the dam of the river.

Would I ever come back here?

She didn't know yet.

They kept walking.

Stones

Sarah Miller

Lee Coombes had a stone his hand, two pockets full of slate chippings and a stomach that had a tonne of rocks in it. It was the only thing keeping him fixed there in the middle of the road, flanked by Tommo and Ackie and almost a hundred and fifty others, some of whom he recognised despite their hoods and the bottom of their faces being covered with their Man-U, Salford and City scarves.

The news had spread quickly across the estate that things were kicking off at the shopping precinct. Someone had already ram-raided Cash Converters and put a few shop windows through and the police were now there in force, cowering behind their riot shields and the cover of two police vans.

Lee didn't want to be there at all. He'd rather be home, shooting up zombies on the x-box but today that wasn't an option. When Tommo texted, you turned up wherever he said and did whatever he and the others did or you'd find yourself without mates pretty quick. And the Langworthy Estate wasn't a good place to find yourself without mates.

Ida was ringing the police again. She'd had an argument with one snerpy woman on the other end of the phone already and was just about to have another.

"Yes, I do consider a load of hooligans coming over my wall and stealing my patio stones an emergency! I paid good money for those and I had to wait for them to be delivered. They were a special order from B&Q. 'Large Plum decorative slate'. I wanted that colour especially and I needed the bigger stones to deter the local cats from using it as a litter tra... .yes, I do understand the emergency services are busy but they've trampled the plants and kicked my corner wall down as well. I rang the community police number first but it seems they're involved in these riots that are going on and are too busy to deal with real crimes that are happening... well, sending someone when an officer is available isn't good enough but I can see I'm not going to get any help from you."

Ida put the phone hand set back on the side table and went to look out of the window again. She was getting more agitated. She could hear yobs shouting at the end of the close but she wasn't going out there, it wasn't safe.

She looked at the mantle clock, twenty past five, and Emma should be home from school even if she'd had to stay behind for a meeting or club. Perhaps she got frightened when she saw the gang of boys at the end of the street and had gone to Carly's? She would ring Carly's and see if she was there. Oh, this was going to be another thing Emma would use to try and get a fancy and expensive mobile phone. It wasn't going to wash but she knew they'd have the argument anyway. All they did was argue these days.

Ida punched in Carly's number and spoke to the answerphone as usual. Was nobody ever in that flat or did they just not bother picking up the telephone? Probably gyrating about and listening to music far too loudly, she thought. Carly and her mother were both 'loud' people who were always bobbing about, shrieking and making too much noise.

She turned on the television and tried to find the local news. At least it would keep her occupied whilst she waiting for Emma and, by some miracle, the police officer who could take her statement and get out there and do their job.

"Ring him again, Carly. I'm getting a cold backside out

here and 'Pervy Paul' has his binoculars pointed at us."

"Maybe we should give him a bit of a show." Carly started singing loudly in her best Beyonce impression, bending and twerking, grinding her body against the side of the wall exposing her midriff and moving her hands suggestively over her jeans.

"Pack it in; he'll be round to tell your Mam!"

"She don't care. She knows he's always leering out of his flat window so she'll only have a go at him for looking at us anyway."

Emma didn't think Paul was 'pervy' at all. He was just old and a bit lonely and she'd never seen him out of his block. He'd go down in the lift to the mail box when the lift was working and shuffle back to his flat on the eleventh floor and put the locks on; locks from the top of the door to the bottom. She'd been close behind him more than once and heard all the clicks and deadbolts and chains being carefully activated as soon as his door shut behind him.

He lived on the same floor as Carly and never seemed to have any visitors. He spent most of his time looking out of the front window and, unless you liked the grey industrial skyline, the large concrete slab that boasted it was 'Shopping City' in big outdated lettering, the shabby terraces huddled and overshadowed by the flats and the patchwork of boarded up and raggy-gardened council houses, there wasn't really much of a view.

The tinny tune of Carly's mobile brought Emma's thoughts back to the present and she leaned in close to her to read the text on the screen.

GVIN COPS CRP AT SHPPIN CTY 4 LAFFS. C U IN 5. T

"Ask him who he's with"

"No way Em, it narks him when I'm texting him all the time. We'll see when he gets here."

"You're his girlfriend aren't you? Why wouldn't he want you to text him?"

"You fancy one of his mates don't you?... Who?"

"Lee's alright."

"Lee! I suppose he's not bad looking but he's a bit of a bottom feeder. Never says much. Dun't even drive."

"Carly, Tommo hasn't got a car either and he spends half of his time round at his exes talking to her."

"Goes to see his kid, that's all. That's why he wants to keep us low profile. She's a bit radgey and she'll stop him seeing Tyson if she thinks he's in love with me... and he might not have a car at the minute but he can always get one when we need one."

Emma knew enough to keep her mouth shut about Tommo's 'ex', that everyone on the estate including Carly knew he was still seeing and that 'love' might be too strong a word for their relationship. She also kept to herself that Tommo's borrowed cars were usually being looked for by their owners and the police as he didn't bother to tell them he was 'borrowing' them. Carly knew all this and didn't want to know or just didn't care.

She was wrong about Lee though. He had plenty to say when he walked home with her the other day. He was funny and nice... but Carly would laugh at 'nice' so she didn't mention that or the fact that he'd told her that he'd like to go to the cinema sometime, on their own, if she wanted to. She did want to. She wanted to see him and talk to him all the time or she wouldn't be waiting to get into a 'borrowed' car and heading into the city centre where shops were being looted and there was likely to be trouble.

Paul turned the radio on and went back to watching what had turned into a huge mob, throwing rocks and bottles at the police. Something was on fire but he couldn't see what; just black smoke and flames rising over the roofs. He was worried about the silly girl from flat 63 and her friend who were sitting on the low wall across from the flats. Did they not know that the estate was a war zone? Did their parents know they were out whilst thugs were rampaging a few streets away?

Radio Salford was interrupting their usual mix of light hearted banter and pop music to report on the riots. The normally jolly DJ was trying to get a bit of gravitas in his voice as he talked about 'violent clashes' and 'gangs of youths in hoodies on the rampage'. He struggled to hold on to the serious tone when he asked listeners to phone in with their eye-witness accounts of their experiences.

Paul was caller number three and he had much more to report than the woman who had to walk to a tram stop on the outskirts of the city zone because they'd stopped trams and buses bringing people in from the outlying areas to join in the riots or the bloke who said he saw kids leaving the Poundshop with armfuls of cheap sweets and cans of pop. He was at the eye of the storm and could scan the whole estate from his flat window.

"So, Paul, you're calling from the Langworthy Estate. What's happening out there?"

"I've seen all sorts this evening. You wouldn't believe it, Tony"

"Tell the listeners what you've witnessed, Paul"

"A family in a blue Nova drove into Aldi car park before and the parents and two kids got three trollies and went in. They came out with them piled high... and the shop closed its doors at lunchtime. Someone prised the shutters and automatic doors open and people have been leisurely looting for a couple of hours now, bold as brass.'

As Ackie tried to find some 'bangin' tunes' on the car radio, Carly shouted, "Stop, go back a bit. I think they're talking about our block on there."

Emma was squashed in the back between Carly and Lee and all she could concentrate on was Lee's hand that was drumming nervously on his knee.

"In't that 'Pervy Paul' grassing up his neighbours live on air?"

Paul was going into great detail about the ram raid and the standoff with the police and the 'hoodies' and how he could recognise most of the estate from their walks alone.

"Stupid or what? He's going to get himself killed saying crazy stuff like that. He's practically given out his name and address. He's just asking to get a sorting. They'll do horrible things to him before they finish with him an' all."

Tommo sounded like he might know who might do these horrible things and what they might be and, right then, Emma wished she was home being nagged by her mother or at the pictures holding hands with Lee in the dark not parking down a back street just off Oldham Street and pulling her hood up to go 'shopping'.

Ida rang and left another message on Carly's machine. It was half past eight and she was getting worried. She's already seen shaky camera phone footage on the news of the police running at a large group of people throwing things at them. She was sure her patio stones were showering the riot shields along with bits of brick that probably came off her garden wall. When the footage changed to grainy CCTV footage of the city centre, she clicked her teeth and shook her head disapprovingly as crowds of people climbed into shop fronts and dragged out trainers and stereos and ran with armfuls of sportswear and expensive looking clothes.

A small figure in a white hoodie and tracksuit bottoms caught her eye in the corner of the picture. Next to her a girl in tight jeans with a bare midriff was pulling a dress from a mannequin. Even from the back she recognised her. Her eyes flicked back to the girl in the white hoodie.

It was frantic as kids on bikes rode around shouting to looters, letting them know where the cops were. It was like a giant game of hide and seek with everyone running to escape the seekers at once.

At first Emma just played the game, moving with everyone else, watching Carly, Ackie and Tommo grabbing stuff as they went, with her and Lee just tagging along but when they got to Carphone Warehouse on Market Street, Carly made it seem like the sensible thing to do.

"Get yourself a phone. Now's your chance to get a decent one. Tommo's mate can unlock any phone so you can just buy a cheap sim card."

"And what will my Mam say?"

"It's hardly a fifty-two inch flat screen telly is it? You can hide it in your trackie pocket."

"I don't know..."

"You can text Lee and he can text you... look everyone's got stuff. Grab which one you fancy."

She grabbed and ran.

Lee looked embarrassed as he walked Emma to her gate. He still had a few lumps of stone from her front garden in his pocket and he wanted to put them back but couldn't.

Inside the house, the two police officers perched on the edge of the sofa looked up as she came in.

"You tell them that thugs have torn up your property and they don't show up but as soon as you say you've spotted your daughter stealing a mobile phone on the TV footage and they're straight round and have time to be waiting."

Emma's face flushed. "I haven't... I didn't." Anger

welled up as she saw her mother's apparent satisfaction at doing what was right.

But a smile spread onto her face when she turned out her pockets. The police looked at the old battered Nokia and over to her mother.

"This phone is definitely not new and I'm sure if your daughter was going to be stealing one, she'd nick a better one than this."

Ida's jaw dropped.

"I've got a teenager," the policeman added, "and this phone is definitely the Skoda of phones rather than a Porsche."

Emma exhaled. She was so glad she'd hesitated at the front door, felt the phone in her pocket pressed against her like a heavy weight and decided to take it to the corner of the garden and bury it. She didn't want it no matter how many texts or calls she could get from Lee.

As she bent down, the sound of stones clacking together made her jump. She thought it might be a cat or other small animal that had got in but then she spotted his outline.

He was emptying his pockets and dropping the small purple stones over the wall onto the edge of the garden. They were both sheepish and awkward but laughed about it after they had spoken.

Before she'd gone inside, he'd given her his own phone, a bit of a 'shed' of a phone but he was getting a newer one off his brother who was upgrading and, at least he'd already have her number.

She had kissed him for almost two minutes before slipping the phone into her pocket and heading inside. Her lips still tingling, the little brick of a mobile, warm and nestled into her thigh as her feet crunched happily over the stones.

Parasomnia

Chloe Hill

Their eyes. I can sense them watching. Watching everything.
No voices, just eyes. I feel them peeling back the layers of my
skin, to the muscle, to the tendons and the bones, they leave
their sticky imprint on the darkness that is concealed within.
Eyes see everything, every detail, every hidden desire. They
open me like a book and devour my scripture. Tracing my
veins like ancestry, my cicatrices their heart lines. Scratching
at my skin I create a show for them, every harrowing fissure a
new exhibit for their gallery. They exist only in the shadows
of the peripheral. They lurk there, they watch, they see me.

Evelyn awoke with a start, feverishly grasping onto the
details of the disturbing dream that had stirred her
consciousness. The harder she tried to recall them, the more
they fell away from her, like the tiny grains of sand that
slowly drain from an hourglass. Disconnected images of
white light and a clinical smell slowly circled away from
her recollection until she was left with nothing but a small
thumping headache in her frontal lobe. Blinking in the light
that pierced between the curtains, she arched her narrow
back, stretching each spinal vertebrae as she went. The
small pops and clicks were oddly comforting to her, they
soothed her somehow. She stretched again, this time
concentrating on each muscle as she went. Trapezius.
Deltoid. Latissimus dorsi. Semitendinosus. Gastronemius.
Her delicate hands held her steady as she swung her legs
from the bed, taking small unsteady steps towards the
mirror. She was greeted by her tiny frame and grey tinged
skin. Running her bony fingers through her unkempt fringe,

she squinted at her reflection. "They definitely look darker." she thought of her eyes.

"An equation is different to an expression—"
Staring at the blackboard ahead she felt her mind begin to wonder, slipping further from the present with each breath she took.
"—this difference boils down to a sign of equality, or an 'equals sign'."
Her eyes began to feel heavy and she was uncannily aware of her diaphragm contracting and expanding. Contracting and Expanding. Contract…

What? When did I start running? Oh god I'm not alone. I can feel them. They're watching. The eyes are there. They're always fucking there. I need to hide, but how do you hide from something that see's everything. My heart pounds. I can't stop though, they're getting closer. I can feel their obdurate presence closing in. The ground is moving quickly beneath me now. They track me like hellhounds, their acrid stench enveloping me, incapacitating my senses. They force me closer to Hades gate. I pass dense thickets that cast eerie shadows over me. I can hear them, Cerberus guarding the ingress, waiting to ensnare. I'm blinking, but it feels reversed. Like I'm opening my eyes and then shutting them again. That's not how it should be. My hands are the same mottled grey, so this is my body. These are my thoughts. I can see a ball of light, I'm reaching forwards. I can catch this. I close my palm.

"Evelyn Wood, does something about Maths disinterest you? Am I to assume you know everything there is to know about algebra?"

111

It had happened again. No forewarning had been given, as it never was. Her cotton blend shirt was drenched through with sweat and her mind swimming with hazy images of darkness and panic. She stared blankly at the figure before her, trying to focus on the words now bubbling angrily from its mouth. Her arm was outstretched in front of her, her palm clasped shut.

"No." Evelyn snatched her fist back to her body, clearing her throat she answered "No, I er, no. I just got a migraine."

The figure stared in disbelief.

"I need to be excused," Evelyn said, sweeping her unopened books in to her bag and bolting from the room. She was uncomfortably aware of eyes watching her.

Once in the corridor she slumped against the wall panting. Every muscle in her body ached as though she had run a marathon. She used the last of her energy to thump her hands against her head then sank to the ground.

"Why is this happening?" she asked the air in front of her. "What did I do?"

"Alprazolam. 0.5mg 3 times a day. Side effects can include sedation, headache and trouble sleeping"

"Trouble sleeping," Evelyn thought. "I already have trouble sleeping. My trouble is that I do it. That it comes and brings the eyes with it!"

"Did you get that Miss Wood?"

"Yeah I think so"

"Good, so like I said, we will arrange another meeting for two weeks' time, when the medication has started to kick in. That way we can assess your progress and make sure this is the right dosage for you."

A smile met her face which she returned awkwardly. Evelyn left the office, feeling no more hopeful than when she had entered. She had seen the way the doctor had looked at her arms. Weighing her as just another teenage mental disorder statistic.

The crumpled white prescription bag stared at Evelyn from the bedside cabinet. The white pills within teasingly calling her name. She glanced over at them a few times before sighing and placing one into her mouth. She lay back and tried to convince herself she could feel the serotonin being produced within her. Fragmented bits of the days conversations drifted into her consciousness. Arousal parasomnia. NREM sleep.

"Nobody got it! It's such much more than a bad dream." she thought to herself as her eyes began to feel heavy.

There are lights all around me, their soft luminescence makes me feel safe, though exposed. I bask in their warmth. I reach my palms to touch them, but they drift just out of reach. Shadows cascading across my face, I inhale their homely scent, scrunching my eyes tight in their glow. When I open them, they have gone. It's colder now. I can feel something in the distance. It's familiar and unnerving. I know what they are without seeing them. But they're different somehow. This time they have come for me. They creep out of the peripheral. They no longer lurk there. They peel back the layers of my skin and leave their sticky imprint on the darkness within. They consume me.

Henry

Christian A. Lea

Henry's face was the same as mine and he was born minutes earlier, which to him, meant he was my *boss*.

I had to ask a stranger the time and then hurried to a phone.

"I'm running late," he said in my voice.

"No *I'm* running late," I replied in his.

"Where are you?"

"Spinningfields. Near Venue."

"Where d'you watta meet?"

"There's a good pub at Shambles Square if you—"

"Not a pub. Not beer. Meet me at that karaoke bar in China town where we spent Chinese New Year once. Remember?"

"You watta go to a fucking karaoke bar?' I sighed. "How long will you be?"

"Half an hour. See you there." Beep.

When I arrived, he was sat alone at a table in the centre. The bar was near enough empty except for one group of drunken Chinese students jeering another group; as one they sang pop cheese in pidgin English. It was the middle of the afternoon but Henry already had two empty glasses on the table and he was tearing into a plate of spare ribs.

"Mr Thompson died," he told me casually, as I took a seat.

"What? When? *How*?"

"Mm," he took a sip of his Long Island Iced Tea, just as another was brought to the table for me. "Couple'a weeks ago. Um, old age. I think."

"Well why din't anybody *call* me? You know? Mr

Thompson dies and nobody thinks I should know?"

"*Fuck*, sorry! I didn't think it was such a big deal, Jesus." He mumbled. "You din't even like him that much anyway."

"So was there a funeral? What happened?"

"You don't have a funeral for *dogs*, Jesus—"

"Why not?"

"*I* don't know, you just *don't*."

"Well… was there a *service*, uh, like a, like a memorial *service*? There must have been a *memorial* service?"

"They took him to um, St Bartholomew's. Injected him with sommit. Burnt him. They spread some ashes over Donald's Row, um, some up at Ormskirk, Stevenson Road. Dad didn't want them so I spread the rest in the weeds growing up the side of his house when he was at the *Bluebell*."

"I can't believe nobody told me…" I complained.

"Well what difference would it've made? You wouldn't 've come back. You wouldn't 've driven to Kath's in Ormskirk and you definitely wouldn't 've taken the ashes to Dad's, so *fuck*, Harry, what difference would it've made?"

"None, I suppose…" I admitted, then took a long hard drink of the cocktail and nearly finished it all. "I just can't believe nobody even *told* me, d'you know what I mean?"

"Are you working?" Henry suddenly asked, taking me by surprise.

"Yeah."

"Good. I'm glad. That's good." He smiled. "Where?"

"Just round the corner. Wait, I didn't know Kath had ever even *met* Mr Thompson, why did you—"

"Kath *bought* Mr Thompson and gave him to us when he was a puppy. Don't you remember that?"

"I thought, uh, wasn't he rescued from the brook? By

115

Blackmore Road? I thought Dad *rescued* him?"

"What? No." Henry frowned; thought. "Oh. Uh, no, there was a *fox* he pulled out of the mud once. But Mr Thompson came from an Ormskirk kennel or sommit."

"What? A *fox*? Dad rescued a *fox*?"

"Yeah, remember, at one of our bonfire parties, a group of foxes surrounded Sam and Katie, so we threw apples at 'em to make them run away? He got stuck in that slushy mud and Dad had to come and pull him out. Then he shot off down a little burrow or sommit."

I frowned; thought.

"Listen," Henry said, dropping the bone of his last rib onto his plate, "listen. Uh, where do you live?"

"Why?"

He shifted from one elbow to another. "It's just nobody's heard from you, you know. Nobody knows what's going on with you. Are you alright?"

"Who hasn't heard from me, Henry?" I almost burst into laughter. "I don't even *know* anybody, so *who* exactly hasn't heard from me? *You've* heard from me. What is this about, anyway?"

"Jesus Christ, would you calm down," he growled holding his flat palm out toward me. "Just calm down."

"...And why the fuck are we at a fucking kara*oke* bar, Henry?" I hissed through my teeth in a thundering whisper. "What the fuck *is* this?"

"Would you just calm down? Jesus—"

"Uh, if people wanted to hear from me, uh, you know, why have I never got that impression before? Has someone sent you to spy on me, Henry, for fuck's sake?"

Now Henry laughed.

"Nobody's sent me to *spy* on you, Jesus, just calm down. I just wanted to see my fucking brother, to make sure you're okay, you know. *Jesus*. You can't just walk away and pretend we don't exist. We're family."

"Hey, I didn't ask to be a part of your family, an' uh…" I trailed off.

"But you are! You fucking *are*. And as your elder brother, it's *my* duty to—"

"Please fuck off with the elder brother bullshit, Henry. You're so fucking transparent. I know you're only here to show off how well *you're* doing, how together *you* are. This isn't a Me thing, it's just another *You* thing. An' as for the older brother shit: stop pretending you're more *mature* than I am. Just… *fuck off* Henry."

He leaned back and sighed heavily. His eyes rolled so far back into his skull that they slipped away and came back out of the other side, locking on to me. He was wearing an Armani *suit*, with a pink *shirt* and a ruby tie clip and cufflinks in the shape of fucking dice for God's fucking sake.

"You need to grow up," he breathed. "Look, nobody's asked me to talk to you. Nobody knows I'm even here right now. They don't even know I'm back in *Manchester*. I just wanted to check you're alright. Uh, *excuse me, two double Vodka and Cokes, please*. Last time I saw you, you had no money, no *job*, you'd left *home*, you know? So I thought you were like, sleeping rough on Wilmslow Road in a *doorway* or sommit."

"Well thanks for your concern," I replied, making careful effort not to sound too sarcastic. "Your *faith* in me is honestly touching, Henry. But actually, against all the fucking odds, I have a *job*, and a place to *sleep* and *money*, and I'm not, uh, you know, destitute on Oxford Street in a cardboard box under the Tramp's Bridge. Not just yet."

In a dark booth at the back of The Siren, Henry bought me a Budweiser and two Jagerbombs as we reminisced about the time we swapped girlfriends to see if they would notice, and they didn't until Henry tried to kiss mine. Then we got into a violent fight that ended with us both at hospital for the night because:

"—you stabbed me with the fire poker!" Henry laughed.

"And then Lauren pulled us apart and you smashed Mum's vase over my head!"

I touched my eyebrow where I still had a little scar.

"You know that really fucking hurt, Henry," I told him, but by now we were both drunk and we laughed.

"I know," Henry said quietly, "I'm sorry. I'm sorry…" and then darkly, "I'm *sorry.*"

"I know, Henry." I replied. He looked up at me as if he was waiting for something. I picked up a Jagerbomb and drank it, landing the glass upside down on the tray. An awesome beat passed.

"Harry, listen right. I need you to go to Dad's."

"Oh, *fuck*, Henry, again? Please, can you just *not*?" I sighed.

"Look, I don't want to *antagonise* you, but I *need* to talk to you about this."

"There's nothing to—"

"I left a box of Mum's stuff. I left a shoebox of photos and uh, jewellery and stuff in the floorboards of my room. Our birth certificates and that."

I sat in silence as my face sizzled.

Henry suddenly pulled out a cigarette and stuck it under his lip and then lit it, even though we were indoors. He held it dramatically in his hands as he spoke, waving it around. It was a prop.

"Look, I had to see you today, *that* was the priority. But my train leaves tonight." He looked at his watch. "I know you don't ever wanna go back there. I know you don't. But that shoebox is all we have of her. We need it."

"I could... break in? When he's out? When he's at the *Bluebell*?"

"Come on, don't do that. You know what he's like. You smash a window in, he won't call the police. He won't even get the fucking window repaired. He'll just live in a draughty house and he'll probably freeze and *die* in there."

"Well, good." I snarled, bluntly. And then, noticing Henry's eyebrows slip backwards, I went on: "Henry, he deserves all of the misery forever and always for how he treated us, because in the end, the love you *take* is equal to the love you *make* and he stirs up nothing but diabolirhea..." I found myself shouting this very quietly.

"Stop being so immature. You're supposed to be *better* than that. You're supposed to be a fucking genius, or summink. You're no better than him if you act like a fucking animal. Be *mature*." He waved the cigarette dramatically. *Melo*dramatically.

"Henry, *please*—"

"Look, just... y'know. Acquiesce, *brother*. Just *acquiesce*."

Piccadilly train station spread out ahead of us. Henry wore his Beatle boots and a Louis Vuitton bag over his shoulder. He gave me a wave and then tangoed into the night.

My head, by now, was a hive of hazy delirium. What he said that night made me feel blue and uneasy, and all I could think of was a phrase I'd read in a leaflet somewhere years ago: *You are not your family.* And I watched his train depart, I watched the hustle and bustle of the station, the people passing whose lives were all as intricately complex as my own, yet when they passed me, as far as I was concerned, they were gone forever, as though they were never there to begin with. I was full of ennui, paranoia, isolation, deepest sorrow and wonder, and I felt *blue*. *I am not my father*. You are not your family.

The Last Storyteller

J.M. Ilmo

You stand on the border. You are still in your world but one more step and you will be in another.

One more step and you will leave the known and secure world where you were born and bred – the only place that you have ever seen – to enter the old and forgotten place which, as the elders say, used to be the centre of the old world. A place envied by all for its might and magnificence; a place on which befell the judgement of the ancient gods and which is now but a vast ruin of a forbidden distant memory. One more step and you will enter the doomed land of the ancient kings.

Once that step *were* taken, you would be overflowed by a powerful feeling of recognition, an irrepressible feeling of belonging. While your eyes would see a vast flat land covered in greyish dust and large craters, your nose would smell no particular odours but the harshness of an ungrateful soil that can't help life flourishing. Your ears would perceive the slight hissing of the treacherous wind blowing continuously from the North, and your skin would feel the bite of the dry, cold, breathless air that surrounds you. But you won't mistake your senses for the reality of your vision. Where your eyes single out a lonely broken stone you will see a flamboyant castle. When your nostrils sense ashes and sterility you will smell fresh bread and a wealthy harvest. While your ears deceive you with a snake hissing you will hear the laughter of children playing in the fields and the crystal voices of women chatting over their tea; as for the lie of your skin, no biting frost nor dryness but the caress of a refreshing wind on a warm, sunny afternoon.

After that promising first step you *would* take a second and then a third and follow your feet towards your ultimate destination. You did not plan this but deep inside you know it – this is the only thing to do – no choice here. Your body walks convincingly towards its goal while your mind is drifting, absorbed by the holy vision of the once promised land.

You *will* go straight across the lifeless desolate land: past the huge craters, past the few unidentifiable ruins, and everywhere that you look you will see but signs of riches and signs of health, signs of life and signs of joy. You will arrive at the foot of the sole remaining hill and you will look towards its summit – your left hand covering your eyebrow to protect you from the inexistent blinding sunlight, your chest proudly forward, your right hand resting by your side, your feet strongly rooted in the ground, standing tall and upright – as dignified as a Roman statue.

On the hilltop you will see fumes escaping towards the sky from a black shape standing out on the naked ground. As you approach you will see this shape more clearly; you will identify it as a habitation, a hut – the only trace of human activity that you have seen since you passed the threshold of the old world. This is the unspoken finality of your journey – inside the hut awaits your destiny. You are finally going to meet the man of the legend – the last living spirit within the doomed land – the memory of the place.

You *are* now just a few steps away from the door that separates you from what you seek. You perceive a slight creaking noise and raise your gaze to observe the old piece of wood –moving... very... slowly... open. An old man steps outside and looks down towards you, with a toothless grin. You've heard strange accounts concerning this man; every story was different but from what you gathered this old man without name who lives on the doomed land is the only soul who can be trusted regarding the tales of the old world. He is said to have been born there – in this very place – all his life – he spent...

He is the descendant from the one who survived, the one who witnessed everything – his last remaining heir. Tales from the ancients kings and their promised land have been told to him by his grandfather... who himself learned them from his ancestors... who have all inhabited the doomed land... and survived there... with this only goal of remembrance. They all lived by one motto, one rule: **The old world shall not be forgotten.**

While you are standing there wondering about those legends, the man on his doorstep waves his hand high in the air with its back turned towards you; he is showing you the entrance before disappearing into the hut. You accept the invitation and after having taken the last steps that still separated you from your destiny, you take a deep breath and cross the threshold of the hut.

The old man is sitting on the other side of a large round wooden table that occupies most of the room. Two bowls of clay are laid on the table, one on your host's side and one across the table in front of a chair drawn for you. The master of the place nods at you which you understand as an invitation to sit down.

The beverage smells of autumn. Steams comes out of it. No words have been exchanged yet.

You open your mouth to thank your host but before the first sound is articulated you see the old man turning his head slightly to the right and blinking both eyes slowly. He invites you to remain silent. You nod in sign of comprehension. You then take the bowl into your hands and slowly raise it in the air towards your host, which gesture he imitates. Carefully, you put the bowl to your lips, feeling the hot liquid passing down your throat – entering your stomach – and – slowly – warming your entire body. When you put the bowl down, you see that the old man is staring at you. He is ready to talk…

Little Red

H. Asran

"Little Red was my name growing up; all the village folk would call me it, to the point where I don't remember my birth name. As it stands now, it's Red. It all came from my mother now that I think back. That superstitious old bat would decorate me with every red dyed cloth she could get her grubby hands on. She told me it was because of what it meant, the colour red was a protection from evil in her family, and it was also hard to come by, so the resale value was high. She was a thief by choice my mother, for me it's all I've known so it's hardly a preference. My mother always told me to do what you're good at. Sadly, I'm a good thief.

My first steal was my ninth summer. My mother and I caravanned out to a trading field a few clicks away from Longtaile. A religious migration, which all females of the Hood family must complete at least every three summers. My mother however, being devout in the ridiculous, opted for an annual visit.

"Your education is at stake Little Red."

"Education?" I would reply, weary from the road and the same old scenic view on the caravan bench, "Is this my in-depth education in the art of haggling?" I'd ask in mock sincerity. She would throw me a look and ignore me, reciting the same tale of her mother and her first migration."

"Miss Red." The bespectacled man-bird stopped her and reached into his right pocket for a tissue. "When I said, retell me the story from your side, I did not mean from the very beginning including your obviously eventful birth." The trial room fell silent, as Red sat there composing herself on the stand. The entire Realm had come out to witness her trial and had listened up until this point with eagerness. She coughed a little and regained her composure.

"If you would bear with me a moment, when you ask for my experience of events, I would prefer if you gave me a chance to truly give me side of it, as I am sure you know, my name has been clouded with a lot of ambiguity." The Queen of Hearts was at the head of the judging panel, she lowered her head a little in silent discussion with the judges. After a moments deliberation she raised her hand and said; "Commence with your story Miss Red, without further interruption."

"As I was saying, my first experience of this gypsy black market, masquerading as a legitimate farmers exchange was not at all shocking to me. Indeed, I knew my mother well enough not to put such effort into attending, were it not such a breeding ground for blood money, magick contracts and, discounted jars of fairy tears.

The road was a long one. So I would practice my singing. In later years, where my singing would reach near perfection, a certain Prince of a certain land would pass by the wood just beyond Longtaile, and there he would hear just a single note and fall hopelessly in love. Of course, were it not for Sleeping Beauty picking blueberries just near him, and he mistaking my voice for hers – well, let's just say, she even had the audacity to not send me an invitation to the royal wedding, knowing full well that she was indebted to me.

It is safe to say it was a downward spiral from the day I visited the much talked about Fairy Grandmother. Upon arrival things started to turn sour. I had apparently been given the wrong time slot and so I arrived much later than was expected.

"I've come to see the Godmother," I said my heart already warm with admiration for her. The sprite gave me a stern look and then recommenced her cleaning of her transparent wings. I flicked my red cape a little to the side, so that my hand lay on my hip.

"Excuse me, little dear, but if you don't give me your full and undivided attention, when I do go into see the Godmother, I'll be sure to inform her of the black-market bug repellent your applying to those pretty wings of yours." She threw back her head in horror and raised her hands in the air, pleading earnestly.

"Well then, if you're so desperate for my silence, you know what to do." She nodded and fluttered towards the army of little sprites behind the concrete walls, leaving a trail of sprite dust in her wake. Just a moment later and I was escorted to the potion vault by two smelly ogres.

"Fairy Godmother!" I exclaimed, wholly delighted to her. She didn't bother to, but I didn't mind too much, she was busy after all, finding some lifesaving potion for some poor little creature.

"I've heard of you Red." She said, finally turning. "And no, not good things, so I'd appreciate if you kept your hands where I could see them." I was hurt to say the least, yet a little flattered by my infamy.

"Dear Godmother, I've not come to steal from you. I'm here to ask a simple favour."

"Then ask it." she said, still eyeing me ever so intently. I brushed it off and walked towards the vast stacks of books on the far side of the vault. She followed after me and ascended one of the ladders to get another book.

"Well, I have this small problem I was wondering you could help me with I have this medallion no safe place to put it, I want to put it in your vault for safekeeping"

127

"Did your mother steal that one?" She laughed at her own comment as she threw various books down towards the ground. I didn't like her much at this point. I was too busy dodging the books she was throwing down at me to notice my red cape had caught in one of the ladders steps. So as I danced about the books hurtling towards my head, and she laughing at her joke, I must have tugged the ladder that had caused her accident.

I call it an accident because it was an accident. I had no conscious part in any of it. The missing potions, books, creams and dyes were not taken from me. However, I will admit to taking her wand, cape and glasses, and reselling them on the market. I have never said I was a liar, only a thief. I hope, now that you've heard my side of the tale, you will understand the passing of the Godmother was no one's fault directly, and not at all mine."

The courtroom was silent yet again and the Queen of Hearts and the rest of the panel exited to discuss the verdict.

Lightning Source UK Ltd.
Milton Keynes UK
UKOW06f0845301216
291071UK00013B/152/P